An unforgettable Hollywood princess in a small
southern town, Divine Matthews-Hardison lights up
Jacquelin Thomas's previous novels
*Simply Divine   Divine Confidential   Divine Secrets
Divine Match-Up*

"There's something compelling about Divine and her amusing take
on life."   —*Booklist*

"Funny, heartwarming, spiritually uplifting. . . . A page-turning story
that's sure to touch lives."
                        —ReShonda Tate Billingsley, bestselling
                                author of the Good Girlz series

"Down to earth and heavenly minded all at the same time. . . . It
made me laugh and tear up."
                        —Nicole C. Mullen, Grammy-nominated
                                and Dove Award–winning vocalist

"A good dose of fashionista fun."   —*Publishers Weekly*

MORE ACCLAIM FOR THE WONDERFUL FAITH-BASED FICTION OF JACQUELIN THOMAS

"Touching and refreshing."   —*Publishers Weekly*

"Bravo! . . . Sizzles with the glamour of the entertainment industry
and real people who struggle to find that precious balance between
their drive for success and God's plan for their lives."
                        —Victoria Christopher Murray, bestselling
                                author of the Divas series

"A fast-paced, engrossing love story . . . [with] Christian principles."
                                        —*School Library Journal*

It's a Curl Thing is also available as an eBook

Other Divine Books by Jacquelin Thomas

it's a Curl thing

Jacquelin Thomas

POCKET BOOKS

New York   London   Toronto   Sydney

Pocket Books
A Division of Simon & Schuster, Inc.
1230 Avenue of the Americas
New York, NY 10020

First Pocket Books trade paperback edition May 2009

POCKET and colophon are registered trademarks of Simon & Schuster, Inc.

For information about special discounts for bulk purchases, please contact Simon & Schuster Special Sales at 1-866-506-1949 or business@simonandschuster.com.

The Simon & Schuster Speakers Bureau can bring authors to your live event. For more information or to book an event contact the Simon & Schuster Speakers Bureau at 1-866-248-3049 or visit our website at www.simonspeakers.com.

Designed by Renata Di Biase

Manufactured in the United States of America

10 9 8 7 6 5 4 3 2 1

Library of Congress Cataloging-in-Publication Data

Thomas, Jacquelin.
  It's a curl thing : a novel / by Jacquelin Thomas. — 1st Pocket Books trade paperback ed.
      p. cm. — (Divine and Friends series)
  Summary: While Rhyann is working as a shampoo girl to pay off her bill for having a very bad haircut and dye-job fixed at the salon Divine and Mimi use, she meets a special person who challenges, inspires, and changes her forever.
  [1. Interpersonal relations—Fiction. 2. Beauty shops—Fiction. 3. Family life—California—Fiction. 4. African Americans—Fiction. 5. Pacific Palisades (Los Angeles, Calif.)—Fiction.] I. Title.
  PZ7.T366932Its 2009
  [Fic]—dc22
                                                                                    2009003591

ISBN-13: 978-1-4165-9878-7

To all who suffered during the Holocaust

You will never be forgotten

Acknowledgments

Thanks to everyone at the United States Holocaust Memorial Museum for the information provided on the history and the survivors of the Holocaust.

A special thanks to my husband and son for your continued support and your patience whenever I'm on a deadline.

it's a Curl thing

Chapter 1

May 2nd

I'll be leaving to get my hair cut and colored for the big day tomorrow as soon as I finish typing in this entry. My day wasn't great or anything—just okay. I'm glad we had a half day at school, because I still have a lot of stuff left to do before sophomore prom. I can't believe it! I'm going to my first prom!

My aunt designed my dress. Well, maybe she didn't exactly design it—it's her version of a Valentino knockoff. Although I go to the prestigious Stony Hills Preparatory School in Pacific Palisades, we don't have benjamins like that. I attend the school on scholarship, and I'm perfectly okay with that. All I want is the end result—a good education so that I can get into a good college.

Okay, I have to end for now. It's time for me to go to my sister's house. She's doing my hair for me as a gift. I'll upload a picture later.

I log off my online journal and shut down my computer while humming to Alicia Keys's new single.

"I'm on my way to Tameka's," I yell as I rush toward the living room, my footsteps thundering across the hardwood floor. My aunt's in the tiny laundry room near the back of the house but acknowledges she heard me by responding, "Okay . . ." Then she adds, "Rhyann, I have to take Phillip to track practice, so I won't be here when you get back."

I grab my hair magazines and zip out the front door.

My sister lives two blocks from our house. Just two blocks in the other direction is the Jungle, where gun deaths are nearly a daily event. My B.F.F.'s Mimi and Divine used to be afraid to come anywhere near here. I used to have to meet up with them at the Baldwin Hills Crenshaw Plaza, but now that Mimi is driving and has her own car, she doesn't mind coming to pick me up. I've told her which streets to take and stuff so that she's not caught in the middle of gang violence.

We don't even go to the grocery store that's right down the street. My aunt would rather go all the way across town.

It's a *Curl* Thing

Bullets don't know any names, she says. A stray bullet killed my uncle when he was coming home from work. He made it to the house only to die in her arms. This happened a few months before my mom died.

"Tameka, girl . . . you gotta hook me up." I hurry through the front door of her apartment with my arms clutching the magazines that are my lifeline to a diva hairstyle. "Do me right because I gotta be fierce when I step up in the prom tomorrow night."

I make myself comfortable on the red leather sofa in my sister's living room, then lean forward to spread the magazines on her glass-top coffee table. Tameka's twenty-one years old and has had her own place for a year now. She keeps it nice and clean—more than she ever did when we shared a room. She used to be such a slob.

"Come help me find the perfect hairstyle," I say to her. "My dress is strapless, and I'm wearing this really cute rhinestone necklace Auntie Mo bought to show off my neck."

Auntie Mo's real name is Selma Elizabeth Winfield. My brothers, Tameka, and I came to live with her five years ago after our mother died in a car accident. She is not just our aunt—she has been a mom to us as well, so that's why we call her Auntie Mo.

"Tameka, I don't want to wear my hair pinned up like everybody else will be wearing theirs—"

"Girl, you know I got you," she responds with a big grin on her apple-cheeked face.

She's wearing way too much blush, but I keep my mouth

shut. Tameka's the sensitive type—she takes offense at pretty much everything that doesn't line up with the way she thinks. Drama Queen should be her name.

"I learned how to do color last week at school, and Rhyann . . . girl, I'ma give you a fresh look. When I get through with you, everybody's gonna be like BAM! *Who did your hair?* When they ask you, tell them to come and see me at McCall's College of Cosmetology." She adds a little pitch. "I'll hook up all those little rich girls at your school. You know I wanna work in Hollywood, too . . . girl, I need to start networking."

I follow Tameka into a kitchen littered with hair products. Well, it used to be the kitchen. She can't be doing any cooking in here, because there's no room for the groceries. "If this is the salon, where do you keep your food?" I can't help asking.

I wouldn't be on my job as the younger sister if I didn't get on her nerves from time to time.

"It's in the pantry," Tameka answers. "I have all this stuff out here now because I have to do your hair, Rhyann."

I turn around slowly. "You're not planning on using *all* of this stuff in my hair, are you?"

She chuckles. "No, but I wanted to make sure I had everything I needed. I don't like having to run all over the house when I'm doing hair."

I relax. This is the first time my sister's cutting and coloring my hair. She's making decent grades in school, so she must be doing a good job. One thing for sure, Tameka has some skills when it comes to styling hair. She's sure had enough practice with her own head. Tameka is forever doing something to her hair. One day it's jet black, and then a few days later, she's got highlights. Right now her hair is a rich, glowing auburn. That's kind of the color I want but a few shades darker.

I remove my hat and put it on the table. "You should've heard all the girls at school bragging about how much their dresses cost. Humph! I don't need a thousand-dollar gown to be fierce. When I walk up in that prom, everybody's gonna turn around and say, *Rhyann Hamilton has definitely arrived.*"

Tameka agrees. "Auntie Mo can just look at a picture of a gown and sew it."

"You should see my dress," I say. "It looks exactly like the one I showed her in that store window on Rodeo Drive."

"She was working on it when I went over there last week. I haven't seen the finished product, though."

I grab a hair magazine and settle into the chair near the stainless-steel sink, ready for Tameka to work her magic. "Beautify me, girl . . ."

Tameka laughs. "Sis, I'm 'bout to hook you up."

She colors my hair while I describe the fierce shoes Auntie Mo found at the Beverly Center. They match my dress perfectly. "Girl, I never thought I'd wear an orange dress, but this one is so pretty, and it looks good on me," I tell her as she gently massages my scalp. "It's not exactly orange—more of a dark peachy-looking color. It's real cute."

"It sounds nice," Tameka states. "I know Auntie Mo

worked it out for you. She made my prom dress—wait, she actually made both of the gowns I wore to prom."

"I remember her sewing the black one you wore your senior year," I say. "It was pretty."

"You should come by here and let me see you after you get dressed," Tameka tells me. "I'd come down there, but I'm braiding my neighbor's hair tomorrow. You're going with Todd Connor's brother, right?"

"Yeah," I reply. "I asked Traven to be my date since I didn't have any other real offers and he's real cute. You know I can't step up to the prom with just anybody."

"Sho' can't," Tameka mutters. "I had me a good-looking date when I went to my high school prom. You remember him. He was fine and all, but he turned out to be a real jerk. He got mad because I didn't want to go to a hotel with him afterward. I liked him, but I didn't like him that much—I wasn't giving him nothing!"

Tameka places me under the dryer and sets the timer for fifteen minutes.

"How did the color come out?" I ask when she comes over to check my hair ten minutes later. There aren't any mirrors in the kitchen, and I can't locate the little one I saw earlier.

"I like it," Tameka responds. "But it's still wet. You won't be able to really tell anything until your hair dries." She leaves the room to make a phone call. Probably calling that no-good boyfriend of hers. I can't stand Roberto because I don't think he treats my sister right.

The timer goes off. I sit and wait for Tameka to return.

Five minutes pass and no Tameka.

I turn off the dryer because the hot air is stinging my neck and temples.

Tameka comes running out of her bedroom a good ten minutes later. "Girl, I'm so sorry. I was talking to Roberto and he was trying to start an argument. He must wanna hang with his boys tonight or something."

I'm not interested in her boyfriend drama, so I hand Tameka a picture and say, "This is the cut I want. This style will look good on me, don't you think?"

She nods. "Oooh, this is so cute, Rhyann. I'ma do it with a razor." Tameka rinses out the dye residue before shampooing me. Afterward she applies a creamy, moisturizing conditioner on the wet strands.

"I'ma leave this on for a couple of minutes. I need to go check on my laundry. Folks around here will steal your stuff if you're not careful. I'll be right back."

While she heads to the Laundromat, located in the next building, I read through the magazine on my lap. I'm so engrossed in my reading that I don't notice my sister's return until she's standing over me.

"I'ma rinse this out, then blow you out," Tameka announces.

I nod, hardly able to wait. I'm so excited about my first prom. It's been all that Mimi and I have been talking about. Divine went to her prom a couple of weeks ago and told us what a great time she had. She even sent us pictures of her and T. J., her date. Mimi and I miss her so much since she moved to Georgia. Her mom is the famous singer/actress Kara Matthews. Her dad, Jerome Hardison, is also a celebrity —and not just for his acting. He's currently in prison for the accidental death of his mistress.

Talk about some serious drama.

I notice that Tameka isn't as talkative while cutting my hair, but I assume it's because she's focused on what she's doing.

Twenty minutes later, I turn around in my seat to face Tameka. The strange expression on her face prompts me to question, "How do I look?"

Without responding, Tameka passes me the hand mirror.

When I glimpse my reflection, I scream in horror.

"I don't know what h-happened," she blurts. "I was t-trying to raise the brown—"

"I look w-whack," I sputter. "That's what happened!"

My hair is a sucky-looking rust color, and one side is shorter than the other side. This is so not the hairstyle I wanted.

"What kind of cut did you give me?" I run my fingers through my hair, pulling the strands, as if this will add length.

"You didn't hold your head straight, Rhyann. I kept telling you to ho—"

I interrupt her, "Don't you be trying to blame me. Tameka, you told me you knew how to cut hair. Girl, you don't know jack!" I can't believe she is standing here trying to blame this on me.

She just messed up my hair one day before the prom! I groan as I drop the mirror on the table. I knew that I should've just gone to a hairdresser and paid the fifty dollars it was gonna cost me, but I was trying to be cheap. I'm so angry right now that I'm shaking.

"I can fix it, Rhyann—"

At those words I jump up and snatch my cap off the table. "I'm not about to let you back up in my head. I'd be a straight fool for doing that." My eyes well up with tears. "Tameka, I can't believe you d-did this to me . . ."

Streams of tears roll down her cheeks. "Sis, I'm so sorry, but I promise you that I can fix it."

"No!" I shout. "Just leave me alone!"

"If you don't want me to do it, then we can go to the school. My instructor can get your hair right."

I shake my head and walk toward the door. "I need to find a *real* hair stylist," I mutter, "and Tameka, you need to stick to doing wash and sets."

Tameka's on my you-know-what list for sure. Angrily, I storm out of her apartment.

She runs out behind me, saying, "Rhyann, just go with me to the school."

I stop walking long enough to respond, "Tameka, if she taught you how to cut, you really think I want her in my head?"

By the time I walk back up to Rimpau Avenue, I'm mad enough to explode.

My life is so over.

My stupid brother Phillip takes one look at me and bursts into laughter. "Why did you let Tameka do your hair? She don't know nothing about hair. That's why she's going to school. Duuuuh . . ."

"Shut up," I yell. Twelve-year-olds can be such a pain. He's too immature to fully grasp just how horrible this situation is.

Chester, my cousin, walks out of our white brick house. He slows his pace to stare at me. "I told you not to let Tameka in your head until after she graduated."

I burst into another round of tears.

He rushes over, giving me a hug. "C'mon now . . . stop crying, Rhyann."

"I can't go to the prom looking like this," I moan.

Chester understands my pain and pats my back. "Hey . . . we can fix this. I'ma take you to a real hairdresser. Tameka meant well, but she just ain't ready for clients."

I follow him to a shiny black 1975 BMW 316, my cousin's pride and joy. Chester bought his baby a couple of years ago from the Cohens, the family that Auntie Mo works for as a housekeeper. He's had it painted and the seats reupholstered, and he's added rims that probably cost as much as he paid for the car.

We make three stops at three different hair salons, but not one hairstylist can fit me in, because they are busy with clients getting prom and wedding hairstyles.

Depressed, on the verge of tears once more, I pull out my cell phone to call Mimi.

"What's wrong?" she asks me. I guess she can hear how upset I am just by my hello.

"My sister messed up my hair and I can't get it fixed," I complain. "All of the hair salons are busy today and tomorrow. Prom is tomorrow night. What am I supposed to do?" I'm sure she can hear the frustration in my voice. "I don't know why I even let Tameka in my head in the first place, especially for prom."

"Why don't you call my hairstylist?" Mimi suggests. "Miss Marilee might be able to work you in today. If not her, one of the other stylists in the shop might be able to do your hair. They always leave slots open for emergencies."

"You talking about Crowning Glory Hair Salon on Sunset Boulevard?" I ask. "Are they reasonable? I don't have your bucks."

"They're the same as any other hair salon," Mimi responds. "Ask for Miss Marilee when you get there and tell her I sent you."

"Mimi, can you just call her and see if she'll take me?" I ask. "We're about to get back on the 101 freeway. I don't wanna have my cousin drive me all the way over there and then find out that she can't do my hair."

"I know that's right," Chester puts in.

I reach over and pinch him right above his elbow.

He grunts in pain. "You better quit or you gonna be walking."

"Please, Mimi," I say. "Will you call her?"

"Let me do it now and I'll call you back, Rhyann."

Mimi calls me back not even five minutes later. "Miss Marilee says she can take you right now. I told her that you were on your way."

I release a long sigh of relief. "Mimi says her hairstylist can take me," I say to Chester. "The salon's on Sunset."

Thankfully, traffic isn't too congested. I settle back against the soft leather of the passenger seat. "Thanks so much, Mimi. Girl, I was gonna have to stay home tomorrow if I couldn't get my hair right."

"What happened?" Mimi wants to know. "How did your sister mess up your hair?"

"Tameka was supposed to give me a razor-cut hairstyle, and girl, she jacked it up. I look a hot mess!" I sputter. "Then she . . . I don't know what she did with the color. It looks horrible. Mimi, I really hope the shop's not crowded when I get there. I'm too embarrassed to go anywhere with my hair looking like this."

"It can't be that bad," Mimi replies.

"Humph!" I utter. "You haven't seen it."

"Then take a picture and send it to my cell. I want to see what she did."

"Chester, do me a favor and take a picture of me with your phone so I can send it to Mimi."

He quickly snaps the picture and tosses the phone to me. "I'm sending it now," I tell Mimi. "Call me when you get it—and you better not laugh."

She calls me exactly four minutes later.

"Girrrrl . . ."

"Mimi, you know I can't go anywhere looking like this."

"Miss Marilee will work it out, so stop worrying."

Chester takes the Temple Street exit off the freeway.

"I'll call you later," I tell Mimi as we turn right on North Figueroa. "We're almost there." Chester turns left onto West Sunset and stops the car in front of Crowning Glory Hair Salon.

Before I climb out of the BMW, I say, "I'll call you when she's almost done with my hair. Chester, please don't take all night to pick me up. I have to get home to finish some homework. Okay?"

"I'll be here," he assures me. "Just call me thirty minutes ahead of time."

Before entering the salon, I pull my cap down low on my head. *I truly look through.* I'm so finished with Tameka.

I step inside the Crowning Glory Hair Salon, surveying the décor. Six stations with black granite countertops are positioned three on one side and three on the other wall. Huge mirrors cover the subtle red walls. Gleaming stainless-steel washbowls are located in the back, near a row of four hair dryers. Clients draped in red-and-black striped capes are seated in black leather chairs. In keeping with the color scheme, all the hairstylists are wearing black attire with red aprons.

"Are you Rhyann Hamilton?" a woman standing at the counter asks. She looks like she should be in her nineties with all that gray hair, but her smooth, wrinkle-free, honey-colored complexion places her around Auntie Mo's age, which is mid-forties.

"Yes, ma'am," I respond.

She smiles. "I'm Miss Marilee. Take off your cap so that I can see the emergency."

I do as I'm told.

The various conversations going on around the salon suddenly come to a halt. All eyes are on me. For once, I'm not looking for attention.

Miss Marilee presses a hand to her chest before asking, "Sweetie, what in the world happened?"

"I let my sister do my hair, and she didn't have a clue what she was doing," I explain.

A couple of clients try to hide their chuckles, but they aren't quick enough. I'm so totally embarrassed right now, I just want to die.

"Don't you worry," Miss Marilee says, wrapping an arm around me. "I'll have you straight in no time."

"I hope so," I reply. "Tomorrow is my prom and I can't be looking all crazy."

Miss Marilee guides me over to her chair. "You're a beautiful girl, Rhyann. I believe you could pull off just about any look—even this one."

I give her a grateful smile before sitting down in the chair at her station.

Tameka will be lucky if I ever talk to her again. I still can't believe she jacked up my hair like this. She's my sister and all, but that girl better not put her hands in nobody's head again until she knows what she's doing. *For real.*

Chapter 2

I survey my reflection in the mirror as I run my fingers through the soft curls. My hair feels silky, and it's back to a warm shade of brown—at least that's what Miss Marilee calls my hair color—but it's short. She had to cut and shape it into a style that is so much shorter than I originally wanted.

Thanks a lot, Tameka.

"It'll grow out." Miss Marilee gives me a reassuring pat on my shoulder.

"I know," I respond. "But it won't grow back by tomorrow night."

My hair is cute, but it's just not the style I wanted for the prom. It took me three long years to grow my hair to bra-strap length, and in one afternoon it's chopped so short that it barely reaches my shoulders. Tameka was only supposed to layer my hair.

Right now life sucks for me.

My depression gets a lot deeper when Miss Marilee tells me, "Correcting your color, the deep conditioning, and the haircut comes to one hundred seventy-five dollars."

Panic like I've never known before fills my throat. I don't have that kind of money. This day is just not getting any better.

"What's wrong?" Miss Marilee asks when she sees my expression.

A wave of apprehension sweeps through me, making me swallow hard. "Miss Marilee . . . I only have fifty dollars with me. Mimi didn't tell me it would cost this much." Pulling at the collar on my shirt, I glance around the salon helplessly. Just wait till I talk to that girl, I promise myself, but right now I can't think about Mimi. I need to find a way out of this mess. "Miss Marilee, can I please work it off?" I ask in a low whisper.

Her light brown eyes narrow. "Work it off *how?*"

She's careful to keep her voice down so that my business isn't all out there, but I'm pretty sure the mortified expression on my face tells it all.

"I can be a shampoo girl," I suggest. "That'll help move your clients in and out if you don't have to do the washing.

I know how to wash hair real good." She doesn't look happy, and I hold up my hands. "Miss Marilee, I'm really sorry about this. I figured I had enough money, but I should've asked you just to be sure. I promise I'm not trying to get over on you."

My stomach is in knots right now, and I can barely breathe. I sure hope Miss Marilee can see that I'm telling the truth. Mimi's got me standing here looking like a bum. She's gone down at least five notches on the B.F.F. chart.

"I don't normally do this," Miss Marilee says at last. "But if you're willing to work a couple of hours each afternoon for a week—we'll call it even."

I jump out of the chair and embrace her. "Thanks so much, Miss Marilee. I'll be here on Monday."

She chuckles. "We're closed on Mondays, but I'll see you Tuesday, Rhyann. Have a wonderful time at the prom, sweetheart."

While waiting on Chester to come pick me up, I watch Miss Marilee work on another client's hair. Mimi likes her a lot, and I can see why. She's a real nice lady and makes everybody feel special. Her daughter China works in the shop with her. She is Divine's hairstylist whenever she's in Los Angeles.

Chester compliments me when he arrives. "You looking good, Rhyann."

"My hair is so short," I say as I get into the car. "I hate it."

"It'll grow back."

Folding my arms across my chest, I retort, "Chester, I don't really care about that. I wanted to wear my hair long for the prom. I'm not going to the prom, because everything is all ruined now."

He answers, puzzled, "Girl, if it was that important, why didn't you just get a weave?"

"If this look cost me almost two hundred dollars, how much do you think a weave will cost?" I ask, rolling my eyes.

Chester glances over at me. "Where'd you get the money to pay for your hair? I know you didn't have no two hundred dollars."

"I'm gonna work it off by being a shampoo girl at the shop for a week."

He breaks into a grin. "Bartering—that's all'ight."

"I didn't have a choice. She'd already done my hair, so I have to pay her somehow."

"You want me to lend you the money?" Chester offers.

Shaking my head no, I say, "I've decided that I'm not going to the prom. I'll just work off what I owe Miss Marilee. Thanks for your offer, but I don't need to borrow money I can't pay back."

I shift my position in the limited space in the front seat. My cousin's going on and on and on about my decision to stay home instead of going to prom. I admit that I feel a little guilty, because Auntie Mo stayed up late making my dress, but all this hair drama has me down. Boys don't understand that a girl's hair is a part of her wardrobe. If my hair isn't right, then nothing is right with my world.

Chester's still running his mouth while I continue to stare

out the window. I'm not about to get into an argument with him. He thinks he knows everything, but he doesn't.

Like get a clue. I'm not listening to you.

I lean forward to turn up the music, hoping that Chester will catch the hint. I don't know why Chester is always trying to preach to me and my brothers. He can't handle his own business. If he could, he wouldn't be having all that female drama in his own life. Chester tries to be a playa but always gets caught up in his own game. He just lost two girlfriends because they found out about each other.

How smart can he be to let something like that happen?

Chester barely has time to park the car in the driveway before I jump out. Auntie Mo isn't home, so I head straight to my bedroom, slamming the door behind me. My aunt had four children of her own when she took my sister, two brothers, and me into her home. Her daughter shared a room with me and Tameka during her college breaks. Auntie Mo's two oldest boys shared a room, while Chester had to share his room with my brothers, Phillip and Brady. Chester got a room to himself when my aunt found out Marcus and Randy were selling drugs and she made them leave.

I lie down on my bed to enjoy the rare peace and quiet. I'm not saying my neighborhood is bad, but since we're so close to the Jungle, we end a lot of our days listening to the sound of police helicopters, sirens, or, worse, gunshots. Sometimes it feels like a war zone. I once overheard Chester telling Auntie Mo that gang banging was so bad that when one of his friends was trying to make a delivery to a store on Rosecrans, a group of gang members approached him and told him that his truck was the wrong color.

I run my fingers through my hair once more. The smooth, silky feel is nice, but I just don't like how short Miss Marilee had to cut it. I shake my head regretfully. This is so not fair.

My cell phone rings.

I don't make a move to answer it. All I want to do right now is just lie here, savoring the silence.

Okay, actually, I'm having a well-deserved pity party. I've had the worst kind of bad hair day.

My pity party lasts for an hour.

Eventually, the urge to vent consumes me, so I snap a photo of myself with my cell phone and send it to Divine, my favorite fashionista. She totally understands how a bad hair day can wreck your spirit. Besides, if I look whack, she'll be the one to tell me.

She calls me a few minutes later.

"Rhyann, why did you get your hair cut?" Divine wants to know. "I thought you were trying to grow it long."

"Dee, you should've seen my hair," I say. "Girl, I looked a hot mess! Then if that wasn't enough, I didn't even have enough money to pay Miss Marilee. I asked Mimi if this was one of those real expensive salons and she told me no. I'm too through with Mimi. I can't deal with her right now. I didn't even call her or send her the picture."

As we talk, I play with the fringe on my purple pillow.

Auntie Mo allowed me to decorate my room in vivid purple hues with sage green accents. Divine and I both love the color purple.

"What happened when you told Miss Marilee you didn't have the money?" asks Divine.

"She didn't go off on me." I'm starting to feel better. "She agreed to let me work it off. I'm gonna be a shampoo girl for a couple of hours all next week."

"Miss Marilee's nice like that," Divine says. "But, Rhyann, I don't get it. Why don't you want to go to your prom? You got your hair done and it looks good."

"Dee, my hair is so short now," I reply. "It doesn't come close to how I was supposed to wear it for prom. You know how long it took me to grow out my hair. And please don't tell me that it's gonna grow back. I've heard that like a million times already."

I blink rapidly to keep more tears from falling. I really wanted my prom look to be perfect. Instead, I let my sister do a hack job on my head, and now everything is ruined. I toss the pillow across the room in frustration.

"Why didn't you just get hair extensions for the prom?"

"I wanted to, but Miss Marilee said that I needed to let my hair get healthy before putting extensions in."

"Rhyann, you're cute, so it really doesn't matter. You could pull off a bald head if you wanted to. You've seen my mom's hair. She's wearing it short now, and I think she looks great."

Divine scores twenty-five bonus B.F.F. points with me

by her compliment. She's a true diva, but she's also a great friend, and she's right about her mom. Miss Kara looks beautiful with her hair short.

"So you really think my hair looks cute like this?" I ask, needing Divine to reassure me once more.

"Yeah," she answers. "Just be sure to wear a chunky necklace. You have a nice long neck—show it off, girl."

I'm not out of my funk yet, though. "Dee, I just wanted to be the fiercest girl at the prom."

"And you will be," she responds. "You and Mimi are going to put everybody else to shame. Now if I was going to be there, y'all would be having issues with me because fierce wouldn't be enough to describe me."

I laugh. "Like whatever . . ."

"Rhyann, don't miss your prom. This is one of the most important nights in our lives. You *have* to go. After Madison and I broke up I wasn't going, but I'm glad I changed my mind and went with T. J. We had so much fun."

I consider Divine's advice. Besides, I really want to hang out with Traven. I haven't seen him much since he started working. He goes to Dorsey High School with my brother Brady, and he's a senior.

"And don't be too mad with Mimi. You know she can be a little spacey at times," Divine adds. "Right now her mind is on the sophomore prom and nothing else. You know how she is, Rhyann."

I agree. Mimi can be very self-absorbed and even an airhead at times.

I can hear a phone ringing in the background.

"Hold on," Divine tells me. "My aunt's calling me."

When she comes back, Divine says, "Rhyann, I need to call you back. My dad's on the other line."

"Okay," I say. "Talk to you later."

I drop my cell phone on the bed and walk over to the full-length wooden mirror in my room to study my reflection.

Divine calls me back ten minutes later, and I can tell that she's upset about something. Putting aside my own drama, I ask, "What happened?"

"Jerome said that Ava's having some problems. She was rushed to the hospital last night."

"Did she have the baby?" It's too early, if I remember right.

"No, they were able to stop the contractions. She has to stay off her feet for the next few days."

"I'm glad it's nothing more serious. She can at least go home."

We talk a few minutes more before hanging up.

I go back to the mirror.

Maybe Divine's right. I could be fierce enough to pull off a designer knockoff and a short, sassy cut. Upon further contemplation, I decide that I can rock this look after all.

Chapter 3

*M*imi, the girl who used to be one of my best friends, calls me just as I'm settling down to watch a movie. I need something to keep my mind off my hair.

"Girl, I ought to knock you slap out," I say into the phone. "I didn't have near enough money to pay Miss Marilee. You had me standing there looking all kinds of stupid."

I hear her gasp of surprise. "What are you talking about, Rhyann?"

"I step up into the Crowning Glory Hair Salon with fifty

dollars thinking I can get my hair done for that. It came to one hundred seventy-five."

She sounds amazed. "I didn't know it would cost that much, Rhyann, since it wasn't a weave. Sorry."

"You better be glad I was able to talk Miss Marilee into letting me work off the rest of the money I owe her."

"I'm so sorry," Mimi says, and I know she means it. "Rhyann, you know I don't ever check prices. We pay much more than that for my extensions, so I figured a shampoo, cut, and color would be loads cheaper."

"Well, everybody doesn't have rich parents like you, Mimi. In my world, we actually have to count our pennies," I snap. "Anyway, I worked it out."

I really shouldn't put all of the blame on her. The truth is that I should have checked the price for myself, but right now she's the recipient of my anger.

Mimi being Mimi, my attitude doesn't faze her in the least. She lives in her own world most of the time.

"Rhyann, do you like the way she did your hair?" she asks after a moment.

"It's okay."

"That doesn't sound good."

"That's all I can say about it, Mimi. It's *okay*. Tameka jacked up my hair big time and Miss Marilee had to cut it. It's so short now."

"Take a picture and send it to me. I want to see how Miss Marilee styled it."

"I already took one. I'll send it over right now."

A few minutes later, Mimi says, "Rhyann, I like your hair. Girl, you need to stop tripping. That cut is too cute on you."

"I didn't say it was ugly." I release a soft sigh of frustration. "I wanted my hair long. That's why I was growing it out. Like duuhh."

"After the prom, you can put braids back in or get some hair extensions—that'll help until it grows back."

Mimi always wears weaves. Matter of fact, I don't think I've ever seen her without one, so she has no clue how devastated I am about my own hair. I was so proud of how healthy and long it had gotten, and now I have to start over. I can't help it. This whole deal depresses me.

"There's no point in talking about it anymore," I go on. "I'm not really feeling the prom like I was before."

"What do you mean by that? Rhyann, you're still going, right?"

"Yeah," I say. "I'm just not as excited about it anymore. I don't like my hair, and that's ruined it for me."

"Rhyann, you look so nice with your hair cut like that. You just have to get used to it, that's all."

"If it was you, you'd feel the same way I do."

"Girl, your hair is still longer than mine," Mimi tells me. "You know I messed up my hair when I had braids. That's why I'm wearing a weave. My hair came out on the sides and I had a lot of breakage from letting a friend braid it. Remember how she braided it too tight? I've been wearing a net weave, so it's growing good now."

I lay down across my bed as the subject of our conversation shifts to boys.

"You know Traven wants to be your boo," Mimi tells me. "That boy is crazy about you."

"Whatever," I mutter. "Traven Connor thinks he's a playa. I don't have time for games."

I'm so not about to get played. Been there. Didn't like it one bit.

"He seems like a nice boy to me."

"Traven *is* nice," I confirm. "But even nice guys will try to play you when all girls got them thinking they're God's gift to women. Traven is fine, but he ain't all that."

"Rhyann, I think you like Traven a little more than you're letting on."

Mimi has some nerve telling me that. "You've already dropped fifty points with the hair drama, but now you've just gone down another five on the B.F.F. chart. *I don't like that boy.*"

She disagrees. "Your guard's up big time, so that must mean that you really really like him."

"Of course I like Traven," I state. "He's my friend."

"You know what I mean."

"Can we talk about something else, Mimi?" I'm not about to admit that she's right in her assumption. The truth is that I'm not sure I want to admit it to myself. The last couple of relationships took a toll on my heart, and personally I don't think a boyfriend is worth all the pain.

"Rhyann, it sounds like you've been taking too many bitterness pills. You need to cancel that prescription."

"Whatever . . . ," I mutter. "People get tired of being dogged, Mimi. I haven't had good luck in the boyfriend department, so I'm quitting before I hurt somebody. Namely me."

"Rhyann, you should go into the relationship just to have fun. Don't take it so seriously."

I can't believe this chick! She's actually trying to give me relationship advice. Every boyfriend Mimi gets, she's planning her wedding after a couple of weeks. She gets too serious way too quick.

"Rhyann, did you talk to your aunt again?" Mimi asks, wisely changing the subject. "I really want you to stay at the hotel with us. It's not going to be the same without you."

I don't like this subject. "Mimi, I told you that she's not gonna change her mind. You don't know my aunt like I do."

"Did you tell her that my mom is the one reserving the room? You don't have to pay for anything."

"She's not worried about that, Mimi. Auntie Mo is concerned more about me getting with a boy."

"We're just going to go from room to room hanging out and partying. Nobody's trying to have sex. Why do they think all teens want to do is to have sex?"

"Mimi, you don't have to tell me—I know all that. It's my aunt who's tripping over this."

"Please, just ask her one more time. If I keep nagging at Mother, she will usually give in."

"Stuff like that won't work with my aunt. You end up with some really hurt feelings if you keep bothering her."

"You can still come by the hotel, though," Mimi suggests. "You don't have to spend the night."

"That's an idea," I say.

Auntie Mo is not home ten minutes before I bring up the subject of staying at the hotel again. We've talked about this almost every day for the past week.

"Please reconsider letting me stay at the Viceroy," I plead. "I'll clean the whole house for a whole month by myself if you let me do this. Please."

"Rhyann, I'm not going to change my mind. You don't have any reason to be staying in a hotel. I'm sorry, but the answer is still no."

I sigh with exasperation. "I just don't see why I can't stay with Mimi and the other girls at the Viceroy hotel," I complain. "You know them, Auntie Mo. *It's the Viceroy.* I'll never get to stay in a place like that. *Ever.*"

"I'm sure it's a nice hotel. I can't imagine why on earth Dean Reuben would pay that kind of money for her teenage daughter to stay in a place like that unsupervised. A lot of stuff goes on at those hotels on prom night. Dean should really keep a tighter rein on Mimi as far as I'm concerned." Auntie Mo shakes her head in disapproval. "She lets that girl do way too much."

"But I'm not trying to do nothing stupid," I argue. "Auntie Mo, I know how to say no. I'm not trying to go there with Traven or any other boy. I thought you knew that about me."

"Going to a hotel ain't gonna cause nothing but trouble, sweetheart."

I fight the urge to have a major temper tantrum. My aunt gets on my last nerve sometimes. After everything I have been through, she should at least let me stay in the suite with my friends. We're not planning to have sex with our dates. They're not our boyfriends, for one thing. Mostly, everybody just wants to hang out, since it's such a special night. What's the big deal?

"Why don't you trust me, Auntie Mo?" I ask.

She cups my chin tenderly. "It's not a question of trust, Rhyann. I can see the potential danger that lies ahead."

"But—"

"Look, Rhyann, I'm not going to change my mind about this." Patting the empty space beside her, she says, "Come sit here with me."

I drop down on the sofa, pouting. I've tried everything else—this can't hurt.

My lips stuck out don't affect Auntie Mo one bit.

"Do you know how many times I've heard teenagers say, 'I slipped up'?" She points toward the door. "Remember when your little friend from down the street found out she was pregnant? What did she tell you when we saw her at the church?"

I bow my head. "That she hadn't planned on having sex—it just happened. She said they just slipped up."

"*Exactly,*" Auntie Mo utters. "Now tell me something—how in the world do you slip up and end up naked?"

I think about Auntie Mo's question but don't have an answer for her, so I stare down at my hands, which are clenched together in my lap.

"Do you think that maybe it was because she got caught up with emotion?"

I shrug. "I guess."

"She told you that she hadn't planned on doing anything. But they were alone in that boy's house and somehow the clothes just slipped off, huh."

Squirming in my chair, I respond, "Yeah, I guess they got caught up in the moment." I hate when she does stuff like this to me. Auntie Mo is always saying that she never asks a question that she doesn't already know the answer to.

"Exactly. Now, what makes you think that you're immune to moments like that?"

"I don't have a boyfriend, Auntie Mo. It does take two, remember?"

"Sweetie, I'm not stupid! I know how you feel about Traven, and I know how he feels about you."

I open my mouth to speak, but Auntie Mo stops me by saying, "Don't bother denying it, Rhyann."

"So I can't stay at the hotel because I'm going to the prom with Traven?"

"Rhyann, it doesn't have anything to do with Traven. You can't stay because I don't think it's a good idea. I didn't do it with my own children, and I'm not going to let you spend the night at a hotel with other teens. It just don't feel right."

I fold my arms across my chest. "Auntie Mo, you're no fun at all."

She smiles. "I love you anyway."

"A car would make me feel so much better, you know."

"Then I'm afraid you're not going to have such a good evening."

I laugh. "Auntie Mo, you are so mean to me."

"Oh, really? Well, tell me this. Would a mean person offer you some ice cream?"

"Butter pecan?" I ask.

She rises to her feet. "I just bought some this afternoon."

I stand up and loop my arm through hers. "I forgive you for being so overprotective."

"And I forgive you for whining," she responds as we stroll toward the kitchen. This is how we resolve our issues—over bowls of ice cream.

Slowing my pace, I react to what she just said. "Auntie Mo, I don't whine."

"Since when?" she asks with a chuckle.

A few minutes later, we're seated across from each other at the kitchen table, eating our ice cream.

"Why are you so quiet?" I ask Auntie Mo. "What are you thinking about?"

"What I was like at your age." She smiles. "I was thinking about my prom and how upset I was with my mother for not letting me wear a strapless gown. I almost changed my mind about going."

"For real? You couldn't wear a dress if it didn't have straps?"

She raises her eyebrows at me. "You know that my daddy was a minister. Both of my parents were very religious and very strict. When your mom told them that she was pregnant the first time, they were devastated. She ended up marrying Robert because it was what they wanted, but that marriage didn't last long at all. They separated shortly after she had Tameka. Monica met your father, but she never told us anything about him except that he was a musician and his nickname was C Love. She was extremely private when it came to the men in her life. When he left, Monica followed him to New York, and that's where you and Brady were born."

"I guess my mom was a rolling stone."

"No, it wasn't like that, Rhyann. Your mama, when she loved she loved hard. She loved your father. She was so brokenhearted when she came back to Los Angeles. That's when she met Phillip's daddy. He helped her get over C Love."

"I hate not knowing anything about my father," I confess. "It's like there's a whole half of me missing."

"I wish there was more I could tell you."

"She didn't have anything in her stuff? No pictures or anything?"

"Nothing that tells me the identity of C Love."

"Was he married?" I ask.

Auntie Mo meets my gaze. "I don't know for sure, but I think he might have been. Back then I asked Monica that same question, and she never gave me a straight answer."

"One day I'm going to find out who he is," I tell my aunt.

"I don't want anything from him. I just want to know what he looks like and if he's a nice person."

"Honey, that's entirely up to you, but I want you to know that I'll do what I can to help. I love you like my own child and I don't want you to ever forget it."

That makes me feel a lot better. "I know, Auntie Mo. That's why I forgive you."

Chapter 4

I wake up early Saturday morning and climb out of bed to get dressed immediately so that I can start my chores. Now that I've decided to attend the prom after all, I don't want anything to mess me up. Auntie Mo don't play when it comes to keeping our rooms clean, and she don't have a problem putting a stop to my plans in a hurry.

"I didn't expect you up so soon," she tells me when I stroll out of my bedroom. "I thought you'd want to sleep in today." I accompany her to the small laundry room located near the back of the house. "I need to get all of my work out of the way before we leave to get our manicures and pedicures. I'm even gonna let them wax my eyebrows." I normally just let Tameka pluck the stray hairs with tweezers, but since all the drama, I'm not letting her touch anything on me anymore.

"Are you excited about tonight?"

"I am but not as much as I was," I confess. "I can't wear the hairstyle I wanted and I can't stay at the hotel with my friends. This is not the way I thought my prom would turn out."

"You can still have fun," Auntie Mo says evenly. "It's up to you. Life is all about choices."

I don't bother responding because there's really no point. Nothing I say will make my aunt change her mind about letting me stay at the hotel.

Auntie Mo drops a load of laundry in the washing machine. "Traven and you are gonna take some cute pictures together."

I can tell by the grin on her face that she's trying to play matchmaker. "We're just friends," I say. *Just friends.*

"That boy don't just want to leave it at friendship, Rhyann. He has a huge crush on you."

"That's his problem," I reply, trying to act nonchalant.

Apparently, I'm not doing a great job of it, because she responds, "I know you, Rhyann Hamilton, and you have feelings for Traven. Girl, just own up to it, 'cause you ain't fooling nobody but yourself."

I wisely keep my mouth shut.

Divine calls me an hour later. "What's up?"

"I'm about to get up outta here in a few minutes to get my nails and feet done. What's up with you?"

"Just got home from my tae kwan do class and wanted to call to see how you're feeling. Alyssa and I are going to Atlanta. We're spending the night with my mom."

"How are the wedding plans coming?"

"Okay, I guess," Divine responds. "She and Kevin are always flying to this place and that place getting stuff. They keep saying they want to keep it nice and simple, but from what I can tell, this wedding is going to be the ceremony of the century."

"I'm just glad I'm invited. I don't want to miss this," I say, excited. "Have you heard anything else about the baby and Ava?"

"Just that she's home resting. She has a friend staying with her, so it must be pretty serious."

"I'll put her on the prayer list," I say.

"It sounds like you're in a better mood. Since you're getting your nails done, you must be going to the prom, right?"

"I'm going," I confirm. "You talked me into it. Besides, it would've been foul to cancel on Traven at the last minute."

"Girl, you're gonna have so much fun. I wish I could be there with y'all. The three divas in the house . . ."

I laugh with her. "Dee, they wouldn't be able to handle it."

"It's too bad that you're not able to stay at the Viceroy with Mimi and the rest of them. Aunt Phoebe and Uncle Reed didn't let us stay at any of the hotels either, but they hosted a midnight breakfast with Aunt Shirley after the prom."

"One of the parents is doing that here, too," I say.

"Are you going to be able to go to that?" Divine asks.

"Yeah," I reply. "Auntie Mo didn't have a problem with that. She just doesn't want me anywhere near a hotel. The thing is that if I really wanted to do something, there's nothing she could do to stop me."

"Don't say that too loud," she says in a fake whisper. "You might not ever leave the house again."

We laugh.

"My mom just got here," Divine announces. "Call me tomorrow. I want to hear all about your prom."

After I get off the phone, I sit down at my desk and log onto my journal.

May 3rd

I was way too upset yesterday to upload the picture of my prom hairdo. Talk about drama! First Tameka screws up my color and then she chops off my hair instead of giving me soft layers. But a huge thanks to Miss Marilee at Crowning Glory Hair Salon for saving the day and especially my sister's life.

She'll never be able to put her hands in my hair again. How could she mess me up like that the day before prom? Deep down I know she didn't do it on purpose, but . . . we're talking about the prom. This is a big deal!

Anyway, enough about the hair. The emergency is over, even though it nearly scarred me for life. I am happy to report that there are only six weeks left of my sophomore year. YEA!!!!!

Almost time for my nail appointment. Gotta go. . . .

Auntie Mo takes pictures of me after I get dressed. "You look stunning," she tells me.

I run my fingers across the tiny crystals hand-sewn along the waistline of my gown. "I love my dress." My gaze travels to Auntie Mo's glistening eyes. "You're not about to cry, are you?"

"Your mama and I used to dream of this day. Lord, I wish she were here to see you." She wipes her eyes with her sleeve. "I wish both my sisters were here to share this day with us."

I glance over at the photo of my mom sitting on the mantel above the red brick fireplace. "I wish they could be here, too."

I reach into my small clutch purse and offer Auntie Mo a tissue.

My brother's prom is tonight as well, but you wouldn't know it the way he's strolling into the house at six o'clock. My aunt's gets on him right away about cutting it so close.

"Brady, the limo is gonna be here in about thirty minutes," she reminds him. "You still need to shower and get yourself dressed. Boy, hurry up."

I run my fingers up and down my dress, admiring Auntie Mo's skills at keeping my mind off the fact that my date hasn't shown up yet. Traven had better not leave me hanging on one of the most important nights of my life.

My eyes travel to the clock set on the mantel.

"Where is he?" I murmur.

I walk over to the window but resist the urge to peek outside. I'm not gonna go all paranoid.

My limo is the first to arrive and still no Traven. He and his parents were supposed to be here by now. I glance over at my aunt, who says, "He'll be here, sweetie."

My little brother, Phillip, runs out of his bedroom, leaving his video game long enough to check me out in my gown.

"Sis, you look nice," he says. "You're pretty."

That's what brothers are for. I give him a hug.

Brady, my older brother, joins us, doing a slow spin before striking a pose, his shoulder-length dreadlocks falling around his face.

I have to admit that he looks decent in the no-button tuxedo jacket and matching pants. Because he's such a muscular guy, this style really works well for him.

"You look handsome, Brady," I say after a moment.

Auntie Mo agrees, before something catches her attention.

"Traven's here and he's looking sharp," she announces, taking a peek out the window.

"It's about time," I mutter. "He was about to get left."

"You need to quit," Auntie Mo responds before opening the front door. She plasters on a big smile when Traven and his parents enter the living room.

I have to admit that Traven looks really good. I love the

seven-button mandarin collar on the jacket over his banded white shirt and black tuxedo pants. He chose a deep peach-and-silver vest to complement my dress. He's got a fresh haircut—I'm loving it. Traven stands at six feet tall, and his teeth, even and white, contrast pleasingly with his dark chocolate skin.

He presents me with a colorfully designed wrist corsage bursting in blooms of purple, pink, and a peachy color that matches my dress perfectly. His parents and Auntie Mo both take pictures of him putting it around my left wrist. The mere touch of his hand sends a warming shiver through me.

Brady suddenly puts his hand over his mouth.

"What's wrong with you?" I ask.

"I forgot to pick up Shaquan's corsage. *Man!*"

Auntie Mo and I exchange amused looks while my brother is having his meltdown.

"I can't believe I forgot to pick it up. It's too late now."

"Brady, calm down," I say after letting him stew for a minute. "Auntie Mo took care of it because she knew you'd forget. Oh, and that corsage you picked out was not gonna work. Her dress is strapless, so you're supposed to get a wrist-let . . ." I hold out my arm. "Like this."

"So what did you get?" he asks Auntie Mo eagerly. "You know I don't know nothing about flowers."

She sends my baby brother off to the kitchen. He returns a few seconds later with a plastic container holding a wrist corsage with mini calla lilies joined with leaves and dark red berries accented with gold and black ribbons.

Brady gives Auntie Mo a bear hug. "I love you."

Traven and I smile and take one final picture before Auntie Mo announces, "You all need to get on outta here. Brady, you need to pick up Shaquan. Then y'all still got to pick up the others you're sharing the limo with. Traven, you and Rhyann have dinner reservations for seven o'clock sharp. You don't know how traffic's gonna be on the way to Pacific Palisades."

I pick up my clutch purse and say, "Let's go."

"Traven, I can't believe you gonna skip out of our prom to hang out with all those snobby rich kids," Brady says. "I don't know why you wanna hang out with a bunch of white folk. You know they won't be playing our music."

"Brady, hush your mouth with talk like that. You don't live in an all-black world," Auntie Mo tells him. "We need to learn to live in unity and not see color whenever we look at another person."

Traven replies to Brady, "I'm going because I want to spend time with Rhyann, and she wants to go to her own prom. If our proms weren't the same night, I would've asked her to come to ours."

Traven takes my hand in his as we walk down the steps to the waiting black stretch limousine. Brady, his crew, and their dates wanted to ride in style in an SUV limo.

"We're gonna have a good time at the prom," I promise Traven. "I know Dorsey is predominately African American, and at Stony Hills Prep there's only about twenty-five of us, but my school knows how to throw a party.

The band performing is white, but we have a brotha for our DJ."

"I'm not tripping," Traven says easily. "Everything is cool, Rhyann."

He and I discuss music and our favorite artists during the ride to Santa Monica, where we meet up with Mimi and her date, Kyle Marshall, at the Lobster Restaurant on Ocean Avenue. Mimi and I always eat here whenever we come to the Pier.

One of the reasons I love this place is because no matter where I'm sitting, I have a perfect view of the Pacific Ocean. Normally, Mimi and I prefer to eat out on the terrace so that we're able to enjoy the fresh shore breeze while we're eating, but this time we're going to have dinner inside.

While we wait to be seated, she checks me out from head to toe. "Rhyann, I don't know why you don't like your hair— it's cute. *I love it.* You look beautiful."

This time I smile. I know from the looks Traven's throwing my way, the evening will work out just right.

We're seated at our table ten minutes later.

I can feel Traven's eyes on me as I scan my menu. "Take a picture. It'll last longer," I say.

He laughs. "Why you trying to be so hard? You're my date tonight, so let's enjoy the evening."

I lay the menu on the table and reply, "Since you're buying dinner, not a problem."

Traven reaches over and takes my hand in his, which Mimi doesn't miss. She breaks into a big grin, showing her pearly whites and all.

I send her a look that I hope says, *Don't you open that big mouth of yours.*

Message received. She picks up her menu and pretends that she doesn't know what she's going to order. Mimi already knows what she's getting, though. She gets the same thing every time we come here.

The waiter arrives. We give him our entree orders along with our drinks.

"I'll have the sautéed tiger prawns scampi style and lemonade," I say.

Traven orders the same.

"Have you had it before?" I ask him in a whisper while the waiter is getting Mimi and Kyle's order.

"I've never eaten here before."

"You're gonna love it, Traven. It's spicy, though."

"You know I love spicy food."

When our waiter leaves, I ask Mimi, "You ordered the jumbo crab cakes, didn't you?"

She breaks into a smile. "Kyle ordered the crab cakes. I ordered the grilled New Zealand king salmon, thank you."

I'm totally shocked. "I don't believe you. You actually ordered something different? For as long as I've known you and all the times we've come here, you've never ordered anything other than the crab cakes. The world is coming to an end—I know it."

Kyle laughs. "So that's why she recommended the crab cakes. She's the expert."

Traven turns to him. "Your dad is Ryan Marshall, the tennis player?" he asks. "If he wins the Wimbledon men's singles title next month—that makes what? Six years straight?"

Kyle nods. "Yeah, but he says this year might be difficult. It's going to depend on which bracket Rafael Nadal is placed into."

"Okay," Mimi interrupts. "No more talk on sports of any kind."

"Then it's gonna be a pretty quiet evening," I say. "That's like saying we can't talk fashion. Speaking of which, I can't believe that chick sitting over there is wearing those ugly shoes with that beautiful gown. Those two things are working against each other."

Mimi takes a look. "You wouldn't believe how much those shoes cost."

"I don't care either," I retort. "No amount of money will make them go with her dress."

Traven leans forward and says to Kyle, "Man, did you see the shirt that guy is wearing under his tux? It's *white*."

Kyle pretends to be shocked. "What? He's wearing a *white* shirt under his black tux? Somebody should call the Fashion Police." He snaps his fingers. "Oh yeah—we're sitting with two of them right here."

I give Traven a playful punch in the arm. "Very funny."

"Oh, go back to talking tennis," Mimi says. "In fact, I'll start . . . Rhyann, did you see Venus on the cover of this month's *Essence* magazine? She looks great."

Traven and Kyle crack up laughing.

We make small talk while we wait for our dinner to arrive.

Our conversation halts when the waiter arrives with steaming hot food. We don't spend a lot of time talking, because the food is delicious. I notice Mimi can't resist having a bite of Kyle's crab cake. She's addicted to them.

After dinner, Traven and Kyle pay for our meals, and we get up and stroll out to the waiting limo. On the way to the door, I catch a couple of haters giving me the evil eye.

Look all you want, because I look fierce and I know it.

Chapter 5

Mimi and I make a quick pit stop to the ladies' room to freshen up before making our grand entrance into the Bristol Room at the Viceroy Santa Monica Beach Hotel. I check my teeth for food particles and run my fingers through my hair.

"You really look beautiful, Rhyann."

I glance over my shoulder to where Mimi's standing. "So do you. I have to tell you, girl, that dress is gorgeous. I know your parents spent some benjamins for that."

Mimi's dress has a crystal bead trim on the halter straps and features a plunging, sweetheart neckline and what my aunt calls a keyhole front. The sweet-pea-colored taffeta material hugs her body like a glove, then flares around the knees.

"Yeah, it's a Jovani design, and it cost a lot. I really had to beg Mother to buy it for me. Can you believe she thought it was too expensive? It's not nearly as much as she spends on those couture gowns of hers."

"And you'll probably never wear it again," I say.

Mimi's mouth turns downward into a frown. "I can't be photographed in the same dress twice."

"Why not?" I ask. "Be original and do something different. That's such a waste of money as far as I'm concerned."

"Rhyann, we should trade dresses," she suggests brightly. "Your aunt sewed her tail off with this one. Your dress is fierce. I can wear that to this charity ball Mother's forcing me to attend with her."

"You better call Jovani or somebody to design something else for you," I say. "I'm keeping my gown. I'll probably wear it to the homecoming dance next year."

"But everybody's going to see it tonight."

"And?" I ask. "I like my dress and I'm wearing it. My aunt worked too hard on this gown just to let it sit in my closet."

Mimi sticks her lips out in a pout. "You're so stingy with your clothes. Divine and I trade clothes all the time."

With a slight shrug, I respond, "I don't like wearing other people's clothing. Sorry, but that's just me."

"You can be so boring at times."

I head to the door. "Back at you."

We meet up with our dates just outside the doors of the

banquet room. We can hear the music—the whole place is jumping!

Traven and Kyle open the double doors so that Mimi and I can enter together. The room is beautifully decorated with luminous blue carpeting and black-and-white wallpaper.

We reserved a table just to make sure we had a good spot when the band performs. Kyle pulls out a chair for Mimi while Traven does the same for me. I can feel everybody's attention on us. For the most part, they're probably wondering who Traven is. All I have to say is . . . don't hate.

After we're seated, Kyle and Traven leave to get us something to drink. They return a few minutes later, chatting like they've been friends forever.

"I really like your haircut," one of the girls from the next table tells me on her way to the dance floor. "Rhyann, you look beautiful with your hair like that."

When another girl compliments me on my new look a few minutes later, I pull out a compact mirror and peer at my reflection. "Everybody seems to like my hair like this. Maybe I need to rethink this."

"I told you." Mimi reaches for her cup of punch and takes a sip. "You look fierce, Rhyann."

Traven wants to dance, so I get up and we head out to the dance floor. I love dancing, and Traven is a good dancer.

On the way back to our table, he tells me, "Rhyann, I didn't know you was this fine. Every time I see you, you got on that ugly school uniform or jeans and a T-shirt or one of your college sweatshirts. You probably got a sweatshirt from every historically black college in existence." His gaze drops from my face to my shoulders.

"I still have a ways to go with the sweatshirts. As for me being fine, Traven, you don't even go there with me. We're just friends and we're gonna stay that way." I'm playing it cool, but I've had to fight the urge to keep from staring at him all night long.

This boy is *fine*.

"Why it got to be like that?" he wants to know, grabbing my hand. "You know I'm into you."

I chuckle. "Traven, you're into everybody. I've known you since I was in second and you were in fourth grade. I know you think you're a playa. We do better just being friends. Trust me."

"Rhyann, c'mon . . . I'm not really like that and you know it. Yeah, I was trying, but then I had to be honest with myself. I'm only trying to do me, you know. My brother is a playa big time. I can't do him or anybody else. Just give me a chance," he pleads.

"You're one of my best friends, Traven. I don't want to lose your friendship. If we get involved and you try to play me, it won't be pretty." I shudder at the thought. "It's not gonna happen. Not right now anyway."

One of my favorite songs comes on, prompting me to turn around. "C'mon, let's dance, Traven."

"I'm not giving up on you, girl," he says as we make our way toward the center of the dance floor.

"Only until the next pretty face walks by," I counter with a smile. "I see you. You can't even dance without looking at all the girls in this room."

He pretends to be wounded. "Rhyann, you know I'm not looking at nobody but you. What do you want me to do? Just close my eyes? Or do you know where I can buy a pair of blinders quickly?" Traven chuckles. "You're crazy."

We dance until a slow song comes on. I turn to walk off the dance floor, but he grabs my hand, saying, "You're not tired, are you?"

"No. I just figured we'd sit this one out."

Traven shakes his head. "I want to dance. I love this song." He gathers me into his arms, holding me so close that I can feel his uneven breathing on my cheek. "I don't think we've ever been this close," he whispers.

I can't talk because I'm enjoying his closeness. My heart is beating with the pulse of the music, and my flesh prickles at Traven's touch.

Hmmm . . . I need to remember this feeling for one of my poems.

The song ends just in time. Another minute and my trembling limbs would've given out.

"I'll be right back," I say. "I need to get some air."

"Want me to go with you?" Traven asks, looking concerned.

I shake my head no. "I'm okay. Just need some air."

I leave him at the table and venture across the room, heading to the door. Outside the banquet room, I take a seat on a nearby love seat.

Mimi rushes over to me and says, "Traven's got you all hot and bothered, huh. I saw you two—"

"Shut up, Mimi. I don't want to hear it."

She sits down across from me. "You sure are acting all evil."

"I'm sorry, but I just get tired of you saying the same old stuff all the time. You know that Traven and I have been friends forever. Stop trying to be a matchmaker. You suck big-time at it."

"You're still mad at me about Patrick, aren't you? Rhyann, he had me fooled, too. I really thought he was a nice guy."

That is the wrong subject to bring up. "Well, he was anything but nice. He had everybody believing that we slept together."

"Why do people always call it sleeping together? You're not sleeping—you're having sex."

I don't bother to hide my irritation. "Mimi, I don't know, and the truth is that I really don't care. None of that has to do with this. Just stop trying to find me a boyfriend. Work on your own love life."

"But I want us to be able to double date. We can't do that, Rhyann, if you have no date."

"Then I can just stay home," I say. "I'm fine with being alone. Besides, I don't have jungle fever, so don't be trying to set me up with some white boy."

I leave out the fact that I do want a boyfriend. I'm just not going to settle for someone who won't treat me with respect. I see all the drama Roberto puts my sister through—I don't need a boyfriend that bad.

"Why are we arguing?" Mimi asks. "This is our prom and we look fierce. We should be out there having a great time."

I stand up and straighten my gown. "Then stop trying to find me a man."

We make a pit stop to the ladies' room to check out our makeup before returning to our dates.

"I thought we were going to have to send for the police," Kyle says with a chuckle. I'm not into white boys, but this dude has some gorgeous blue eyes. He's fine, I can't deny that. He and my girl really look good together.

I glance over at Traven and grin. "Did you miss me?"

"You know I did."

My heart flutters in response to his smile.

After the dance, we all pile into our cars and head to an oceanfront estate where the parent of one of my classmates is hosting a late-night breakfast for us.

Traven whistles softly. "Man, they living large up in here."

"Who needs this much house?" I whisper. "And it's sure got a lot of glass walls. I bet it's hard to keep it cool in here during the summer months."

He's looking all around, amazed. "What do her parents do?"

"I think her father is an entertainment lawyer, and her mother used to be a soap opera actress. She writes children's books now."

"Cool . . ."

"We could put both of our houses in here," I say, nudging him. "Actually, I think we could fit my whole block right here in the ballroom. Can you believe this, Traven? They have a *ballroom.*"

"I just heard somebody say that they have their own movie theater downstairs. Plus an indoor tennis court."

"I believe it," I respond. "Sugar's on the tennis team and she's really good."

Traven gives me a wry look. "Who names their child Sugar?"

"Rich people."

We laugh.

Sugar walks over to us. "Rhyann, I'm so glad you could come. I don't see you much outside of school."

"Girl, that's because we don't travel in the same circles. See, I live in the hood with the real folks and well . . . you're here amongst the beautiful people."

She laughs and runs her fingers through long blond hair. "Rhyann, you're so funny. I know where you live and it's not in the hood."

It's real close to the hood, I want to say. "Anyway, thanks for inviting me. Sugar, your house is huge, girl."

She looks apologetic. "I know. I keep telling my parents that we should find something smaller. It's just the three of us and the staff. I told Mother just yesterday that there are rooms I've never been in."

"For real?"

She nods. "I'm sure there are. This house is over twenty-five thousand square feet. It's a warehouse for antiques."

I can't believe that Sugar doesn't like her house. I do think it's way too much house for me. I just want a fierce condo when I grow up. I don't need all this.

"She's pretty cool," Traven says when Sugar moves on to greet more of her guests.

"Yeah, she is," I respond.

Traven and I get in line for the breakfast buffet.

"Man, this is something," he whispers. "Look at all this food. I'm not gonna be able to sleep after eating this stuff."

Sugar's parents went all out. There are three types of scrambled eggs, huge fluffy Belgian waffles, pancakes, turkey sausages, beef sausages, bacon, cereal, fruit, and a chef to prepare omelets. Traven and I both decide to try a seafood omelet after Mimi orders one.

"You're going to love it," she tells us.

My mouth waters as I watch the chef gently push the cooked portions of egg white mixture toward the center. When the eggs are set, but moist, he sprinkles cheese and spoons chunks of lump crabmeat and shrimp over half of the omelet. Truly focused on what he's doing, he cooks two at a time. When the omelets are ready, he folds them in half and slides them onto warm plates.

Traven has more of an open mind, because he's asked the chef to add mushrooms and chopped green onions to his omelet. I'm just sticking to the seafood for now. I want to see how this works out first.

We dive into our food as if we haven't eaten in days. Dancing can give you an appetite.

"Where's Traven?" Mimi asks after a while, taking a seat beside me.

I steal a quick peek over my shoulder. "He's ordering another seafood omelet. I think you started something, Mimi."

She breaks into a grin. "I told you it was delicious."

It's a different taste to me, but it's not bad. I can't say, though, that I'll be ordering another one anytime soon.

When Traven and I finish eating, I check my watch, noting the time. We need to be heading home pretty soon in order for me to make my curfew. Auntie Mo extended it because it was prom night, so I want to be home on time. This way I can make a case to have her extend it permanently.

"Rhyann, I really wish you were coming back to the hotel with us," Mimi says when I walk over to her to say good-bye. "Why don't you and Traven come by for a little while? We're just going to listen to music and dance."

I shake my head. "No, I'm going home. I don't want to get to the hotel and then have to leave a few minutes later."

She gives an understanding nod. "I'll give you a call tomorrow then."

We hug. "Have fun and stay out of trouble," I say.

"I will."

"How come you're not going to that fancy hotel with your friends?" Traven questions as we walk out to the waiting limo.

"My aunt wouldn't let me."

When he doesn't respond, I say, "Why? Did you want to go by there?"

Traven shrugs nonchalantly. "I just wanna spend time with you. Besides, we can do the same thing in the limo that we'd do in a hotel room."

I can feel my back stiffen. I can't believe that Traven just said that to me. Nothing is jumping off in this limo. I shouldn't be surprised, though. I knew all along that he was nothing more than a playa.

I take a deep breath and release it slowly.

"Hey, are you okay?" Traven inquires.

I nod. "Just getting tired."

What I'm really tired of is boys that are constantly trying to get over on me. Or should I say, get on top of me. That's not at all what I'm looking for in a relationship.

"I thought maybe we could just ride around for a little while," Traven offers. "We could—"

I cut him off. "No, I want to go straight home."

Traven peers at my face. "You sure you're okay?"

"I'm fine."

"You look like you're upset about something."

"I'm really tired," I respond.

He attempts to start a conversation with me, but right now I don't really have any words for Traven. I'm still dealing with the fact that he really tried to play me tonight.

"Hey, I got my acceptance letter to North Carolina State University today."

I glance over at him. "Congratulations," I say flatly. "I'm happy for you."

I'm really excited for him, but I'm disappointed and upset

that he actually thought I would have sex with him—and in a car, of all places.

He places his arm around me. "You know, just because I'm going to N.C. State doesn't mean we can't be together."

I can feel my body stiffening. "That's all the more reason why we're not getting together. I don't like long-distance relationships."

"Have you ever been in one?"

I give him a fish eye. "I'm finishing up my tenth-grade year. We just left the sophomore prom, remember?"

"I keep forgetting how young you are. I guess it's because you always act so much older."

"I prefer 'mature' to 'older,'" I respond. "And you're only two years older than me, okay?"

"Oh, excuse me," he corrects himself. "'Mature' is what I meant to say. I'm not complaining, though. I like that about you."

"I thought you liked the fact that I taught you how to ride your bike but I had your friends thinking you were teaching me."

He laughs at this old memory. "Girl, they would've ragged on me for days. I had this brand-new bike but was afraid to ride it. I don't know why my dad just assumed I knew how to ride. I guess most boys in our neighborhood did, so he thought I did, too. My mama never learned how to ride, so she couldn't teach me. Todd was real sick back then."

Traven's dad worked two jobs from the time I met them until a couple of years ago. I'd heard it was because he was paying off Todd's hospital bills. Traven's brother almost died after he got blood poisoning. Auntie Mo always said that it was the power of prayer that kept him alive.

Traven's dad only works one job now, but even when he's off, he won't sit still too long. He's always keeping himself busy. He spends a lot of time with Traven and his brother, Todd. Trying to make up for all the lost time, I'm thinking.

I recall a funny part. "I felt so bad for you, so I took you to Auntie Mo's backyard and taught you how to ride. I don't think my aunt appreciated you trashing her flower garden, though."

"I bought her some more flowers, remember? Me and my mom brought them over to the house."

"Oh, yeah . . . that's right."

Traven's eyes travel to my face. "Rhyann, I had a great time with you tonight. Thanks for taking me to your prom." In a surprise move, Traven leans forward and kisses me. "Next time ask me if I want your lips on me."

"I can't believe you just did that," I say, my lips still warm and moist from his kiss.

"I've wanted to do that for a long time, and this seemed like the perfect time. Hey, we are on a date." Seeing I'm not pleased, Traven's smile disappears. "I hope I didn't offend you."

The air is filled with expectancy.

I clear my throat loudly in my sudden nervousness. It's not my first kiss or anything. I wouldn't have minded so much, but knowing that Traven had planned on trying to get with me kind of spoiled this kiss. He's just trying to add another fool to his conquest list.

"Why are you so quiet?" Traven asks, gathering me into his arms.

"I'm thinking," I respond, pushing away from him. It's the truth, so why try and cover it up?

"About?" he prompts.

"Everything you've said to me, Traven. It's a lot to think about."

Traven looks at me tenderly. "I really like you, Rhyann."

Yeah, right.

"You don' have anything to say?" Traven asks.

"I need time to really sort this out."

He nods. "Okay."

"Just like that?" I expected him to fight me on this. At least that's what the other boys have done in the past. They tell you exactly what you want to hear and then WHAM! You're in love and doing everything you can for your man while he's laughing about you with his friends.

"What do you want me to say?" Traven asks. "I care about you and I'm not going anywhere."

The limo slows down to a stop in front of my aunt's house.

"Bye, Traven," I say, reaching for the door handle.

"My job isn't done yet. I still have to walk you to the door."

The driver gets out and opens the door for me.

"Thank you," I say to him.

Traven gets out behind me. "My mama raised me right."

He escorts me up the steps.

We say our good-byes before I turn to unlock the front door. Traven stands near the stairs, making sure I get inside safely. His mama definitely raised him right.

I glance back over my shoulder and give him a wave before closing up. Confused, I close the door as quietly as I can. What is up with this dude?

"I hope you had a wonderful time at the prom," Auntie Mo says from the chair in the darkened living room.

"I knew you were still up," I tell her. "Are you planning on staying up until Brady comes home, too?"

She yawns. "He'd better be coming through those doors in another twenty minutes. You have fun?"

"I did. Everything was so nice. I'll tell you about it in the morning."

Auntie Mo stretches and yawns a second time. "Okay, baby. Good night."

"Good night, Auntie Mo."

I don't get undressed after slipping into my room. Instead, I sit down on the edge of the bed trying to figure out Traven. This dude has skills. He almost had me convinced that he really cared for me. But it's just a game to him. He showed his hand when he assumed we would be getting it on in the limo.

A tiny smile tugs at my lips. *I played him.* Traven thinks I'm falling for his game, which couldn't be further from the truth.

No way that's happening.

Chapter 6

$\mathcal{M}$orning comes excessively early for me. I didn't get home until 1:30 a.m. and I'm still sleepy, but I know Auntie Mo's not gonna let me miss church just because of prom.

After a quick shower, I jump into a pair of black pants and a fuchsia-colored top and head to the dining room, where Auntie Mo has already laid out a spread.

"Good morning," I say, taking one of the empty chairs at the table. My brothers are still in their room. Those boys are always the last ones to get ready.

"Did you have a good time?" Chester asks while pouring himself a cup of coffee.

"I did," I confirm with a smile. "Traven and I stayed on

the dance floor. The band wasn't all that, but our DJ was off the hook." I pick up my plate and begin loading it down with scrambled eggs, bacon, and a piece of toast.

"Like I was saying," Chester says to my aunt, "Brady has to choose the right college, one that will put his education first and not his athletic ability."

I guess I walked into the middle of their conversation concerning my brother. Brady could already have a full ride, but Chester and Auntie Mo are advising him to take time to research each school thoroughly. He's really waiting to hear back from the University of Southern California, home of the Trojans. That's his first pick, but if it doesn't happen, they are looking at a couple of other schools.

The funny thing is that Chester hasn't spent day one in a college, but he's determined to have me, Brady, and Phillip go. He was upset that Tameka didn't want to attend college. He finally stopped nagging her after she decided on cosmetology school.

I'm almost done eating by the time my brothers join us.

While we eat, Brady brags about what a great time he and Shaquan had at their prom.

As if anybody here cares.

"I can't wait to see your prom pictures," Auntie Mo tells me. "I know they're beautiful."

"I hope so," I say. "My hair wasn't the way I wanted it, but it still looked good, I guess."

After breakfast, we clean up and prepare to leave for church. I rush back to my room to make sure every strand is in place and that my outfit is totally together. I have to represent even in the house of the Lord.

Tameka's already there by the time we arrive at Faith Christian Church. I'm still upset with her, so I'm not in the mood for sisterly chatter.

"Your hair looks real cute, Rhyann," she tells me—her attempt to make conversation. "I'm so sorry about everything."

I don't respond.

"I hope you had a good time at your prom. I feel bad for messing it up for you."

I meet her gaze straight on. "You didn't mess up my prom, Tameka—just my hair."

Her eyes fill and she looks like she's about to cry, so I say, "I know you didn't do it on purpose, Tameka."

"I'm so sorry."

"We're cool," I tell her, wrapping my arms around her. "But just so you know, until I'm sure that you know what you're doing, you're not putting your hands back in my head."

Tameka gives a slight nod. "I guess I deserve that."

I almost feel bad for saying that, but when I think about what she did to me, I'm not feeling *that* sympathetic. I excuse myself and leave the sanctuary to join some of my friends in the administration building.

I find them sitting in one of the empty classrooms talking about a girl that recently left the praise team.

"How was your prom?" one of the girls asks.

"Great," I respond. "I had a good time." I take a seat in an empty chair and ask, "Do you know when they're going to replace Ashley?" There is only one slot available, and four of us want to be on the team.

"I heard that there's going to be tryouts in a couple of weeks," another girl answers. "Are you going to audition?"

"I'm thinking about it." My only hesitancy is that one of the persons interested is Kelly, a friend of mine. She and I are not as close as me and Mimi or me and Divine, but we're close. I know she wants to be on the praise team as much as I do.

I'm not trying to lose friends over this.

I hang out with the girls until I see the choir members start to line up for their entrance into the sanctuary.

Standing up, I say, "I'd better head inside before my aunt comes hunting me down."

Inside the sanctuary, I sit down between Auntie Mo and Tameka in our usual spot, the fourth row. My aunt wants to make sure we don't ever miss a word of Pastor Scott's sermons.

When service ends, we slowly exit the church, stopping here and there to talk with other members and friends.

"What was up with Pastor Scott and all that Jewish stuff he was talking about?" I ask my aunt as we climb into her van. My brothers are riding home with Chester, so it's just the two of us in her car.

She shrugs. "I don't know, but it was a good sermon, I thought."

"It was interesting," I admit. "Especially when he mentioned the part about the woman with the issue of blood and how touching the hem of Jesus' garment was so significant. All she had to do was touch his robe and she was healed. That's totally cool."

"She had to have faith, Rhyann. She had great faith."

"I still think it's cool to be healed just like that," I respond. "When Pastor Scott was talking about it, he almost had me up there shouting."

Auntie Mo chuckles. "You need to quit, Rhyann. You weren't about to be up shouting nowhere. The spirit don't just fall on you just like that."

"Are you sure?" I ask. "Sister Hargrove sure be slain in the spirit every Sunday she in church. Around the same time, too. Watch next Sunday . . . at five minutes to twelve—she'll be falling out."

"Rhyann . . ." My aunt can't finish her sentence because she's laughing too hard. "You wrong."

"It's the truth and you know it," I respond with laughter. "You just don't want to say it. Auntie Mo, you're always telling me confession is good for the soul, so c'mon and tell the truth. Sister Hargrove don't always have to be slain in the spirit, do she?"

"I don't know. You'd have to ask her."

"Well, I don't think so." I change the subject back to the sermon. "Auntie Mo, I just can't imagine having a sickness like that for twelve long years."

"I can't either. She didn't just suffer physically, though,

Rhyann. This woman had to have suffered emotionally as well. And like Pastor Scott said, she suffered spiritually. Can you imagine seeking God and praying for Him to heal you of your illness for twelve years?"

"I don't know if I'd still have any faith left," I admit. "It doesn't take God twelve years to do anything unless He wants it to be that way."

"When something like that happens, perhaps He's showing us something," Auntie Mo says. "Or He could be teaching us. Our time is not God's time, and we can never know the mind of God. His thoughts are far greater than we could ever comprehend."

"That woman had it bad, though, Auntie Mo. Pastor Scott said that back then a woman was considered unclean during her menstrual cycle—well, this chick had one for twelve years."

"She was considered unclean for all that time. She couldn't be around her own family. And she couldn't be in the Temple, so not only was she ostracized by everyone, she couldn't go to church. That poor woman had to be spiritually starved."

I shake my head. "That's messed up."

"That's what Pastor Scott meant about us being thankful for what Jesus did for us. Because of Him, we can come to church in any shape or form. We can come to Him just as we are."

I nod in agreement. "I'm sure glad times have changed."

"Praise the Lord," Auntie Mo says.

As soon as we get home, she starts barking orders. Divine calls this Mom Mode, but I call it straight Military Mode.

"Brady, go tell your brother that he needs to make sure he has clean clothes for school," Auntie Mo tells him. "I don't remember seeing any of his laundry when I did the washing. If he don't have any, then he needs to get busy."

"Yes, ma'am."

Tameka enters the house. "Hey, everybody."

"I should've known you'd be coming around," I say. "Girl, you need to bring some groceries since you're over here every Sunday for dinner."

"I love you, too," she replies.

Tameka hugs our brothers, then she and Brady lapse into a light banter.

I interrupt their conversation by saying, "Tameka, if you're planning to eat dinner with us, then you need to help in the kitchen."

She gives a short sigh. "I came down here to get a break from cooking."

"Yeah, right," I utter. "Like you actually been cooking. The only thing I've seen in your kitchen lately is hair products."

Tameka glances over at Auntie Mo and asks, "Where is the love?"

We laugh.

"Did you have a good time last night?" Tameka inquires.

I nod. "The band was good, but our DJ was fierce."

She and I head to my room to talk while I change out of the clothes I wore to church. I'm going to be helping Auntie Mo with the cooking, so I slip on a pair of denim shorts and a blue-and-white T-shirt.

"I think you and Traven make a cute couple," Tameka states. "Are you interested in him at all?"

"He and I have been friends for over ten years. I don't think we'll mess it up by getting involved." Checking them, I run my fingers through the bouncy curls. My hair is holding up well—Miss Marilee knows her stuff. "How are you and Roberto? I know that you were having some issues."

"Girl, he is getting on my last nerve. I told him last night that we need some time apart. I'm tired of his lying tail."

I've heard this story before. Tameka knows she's not about to break up with that jerk. She'll be mad for a few days and then it'll be back to all lovey-dovey between those two. Auntie Mo doesn't even want to hear about their drama anymore. She gets mad when Tameka talks about how Roberto disrespects her, and then, when things are good between them again, Auntie Mo is still mad.

I respect myself too much to deal with a jerk. I guess that's why I don't have a boyfriend. Sometimes drama beats being lonely, though.

Tameka and I venture to the kitchen to help Auntie Mo with the Sunday dinner. She's cooking one of my favorites—drunken chicken, rice, collards, and corn-bread muffins. Making the muffins is always my job. Tameka may not be able to do hair, but she can throw down on some greens. She makes them nice and spicy. Roberto is a head chef at a restaurant that specializes in New Orleans cuisine, and he gave her some tips.

Before we left for church, Auntie Mo dropped a seasoned

whole hen into the Crock-Pot, then added chopped green onions, chopped red and green bell peppers, and cooking sherry. I guess that's why the chicken is drunk.

I savor the smell of the cooking meat and can hardly wait until it's ready.

"Auntie Mo, are you working on Thursday?" Tameka asks.

"I think so," she responds. "I have a doctor's appointment on Wednesday, so I switched with one of the other girls. What's going on?"

"I wanted you to go with me to this furniture store. I need to buy something for that second bedroom, and they have some futons on sale."

"We can go Wednesday if you want."

"I have class all day," Tameka says.

The telephone rings, cutting into their conversation. The phone call doesn't last long, but my aunt's mood heads straight south.

"What's wrong with you?" I ask my aunt when she gets off the phone. "You look like you're about to blow over something."

"That Gloria Cohen is getting on my last nerve," she mutters, pacing back and forth. "Jesus, lover of my soul . . . You are my rock and my strength . . ."

I can tell she's angry because she gets all red in the face and starts spouting scriptures.

Auntie Mo finally stops. "She wants me to work all day tomorrow and then help with her dinner party tomorrow night. Like I don't have nothing else to do."

"Did you tell her no?" Tameka asks.

She shakes her head. "I didn't really tell her anything other than I'd have to call her back." Auntie Mo folds her arms across her chest. "I can't stand this last-minute stuff she tries to pull. People like her really think they own the world. They think all they got to do is say jump and we supposed to say how high."

I nod in agreement. My aunt's been working for the Cohen family for over ten years as their housekeeper. They always want her to help when they throw parties. You can't blame them, though. She can throw down in the kitchen.

"I'm gonna have a long talk with Gloria and that husband of hers," Auntie Mo vows. "And if I do this for them, I better see some overtime in my check. I don't work for free."

"I know that's right," I respond. "Tell them to pay you time and a half, Auntie Mo."

"Oh, they not gonna do that. They cheap as all get-out. I am gonna tell them that slavery days are long over. If I work, they paying me for my time or I'll go out there and find me another job. They have been pretty decent to me over the years, but I can't let them keep taking advantage of me. People are always saying how cheap Jews can be. I try not to think that way, but right now I'm inclined to agree with the consensus."

"I still think they should pay you more money."

She laughs. "So do I, Rhyann. But Abraham Cohen ain't gon' pay any more than he has to—that's just the way it is. If I hadn't put my foot down in the past, I'd still be getting paid same as when I first started working for them."

Chester and Phillip walk into the room.

"We going down to Marcus's apartment for a minute," Chester announces. "He bought some spikes for Phillip. They're the Nike Rival ones he wanted."

Auntie Mo grunts but doesn't say a word.

Marcus is just trying to get back on my aunt's good side through my brother, but from the looks of it, it's not gonna work.

By the time dinner is ready, they still aren't back.

"Well, we're not waiting on them." Auntie Mo fixes plates for the three of us.

I say the blessing once we're all seated at the table.

"You put your foot in this chicken," Tameka says. "It's delicious."

I agree. I'm not doing too much talking, because I'm stuffing my face.

"Hey, Rhyann, are you gonna audition for the praise team?" Tameka asks.

I take a sip of water. "I'm thinking about it. You know Kelly is trying out."

"Oh, I didn't know that," my sister responds. "Well, I hope you get it."

"Me too." I've been wanting to join our praise team for a long time. Kelly is my girl, but she trips out when she doesn't get her own way.

When we're done eating, we clean up, then settle into the family room to watch some television.

I pick up the photo of my mother from the end table. I

was six years old when she died in a car accident, so I have snatches of memories of her, but Phillip was only two and doesn't remember her at all.

"You look just like her."

I turn around to face my aunt. "You really think so?"

She nods. "You have her dimples, her eyes, and her nose."

"She was so beautiful," Tameka murmurs as she drops down into the olive-colored leather love seat.

"She and Cherise looked like our mother," Auntie Mo notes. "Tameka, you look a lot like my father. Both you and Tanya."

"People usually think Tameka and Tanya are sisters," I say. "Because they look so much alike."

"I know how much you both miss your mother and Cherise," my aunt says. "Lord knows I miss my sisters, too. When we were growing up, we weren't close. It wasn't until Monica graduated high school that she and I became almost inseparable."

My eyes travel over to the folded flag in the wooden display case. "I don't think it's fair that God takes both my mom and Aunt Cherise like that," I say, taking a seat beside Auntie Mo.

"Baby, I understand how you feel," Auntie Mo responds. "I felt the same way when your grandparents died and when I lost my husband."

"I know people die all the time, but it just seems like our family has seen so much death."

Auntie Mo agrees. "Death is a part of life, sweetheart. It's the one thing none of us can ever escape. That's why it's so important not to waste one moment of the time you've been given."

We hear the sound of a helicopter overhead.

Auntie Mo stirs, looking toward the window. "Lord, where is my son? I hope he doesn't get caught up in some shoot-out. I can't go through that again. And I hope Brady is with them and not hanging out on some corner."

"I'm in my room," Brady yells out. "Phillip went with Chester."

"Why didn't you come to the dinner table when I called you?" Auntie Mo demands. "How long you been in the house?"

"I've been home since we came in from church. I was asleep until a few minutes ago," Brady answers. "I heard y'all in there talking when I went to the bathroom."

"Boy, you were in that room running your mouth with that girl," I say when Brady joins us in the family room.

Brady gives it right back to me. "You should've asked Chester to drop you at the mall so that you could buy yourself a life."

"And you need to go out and find yourself some sense, because if you call yourself going with Shaquan, you've really lost your mind. That girl is nothing but trouble. I told you what happened with Divine's cousin. Chance is doing double duty as a father and trying to finish up high school."

"I'm not Chance," Brady states. "I'm not gonna get caught up like that."

Jacquelin Thomas

"You better not," Auntie Mo chimes in. "I'm not taking care of another child. I've done all the raising of children I intend to do. I didn't mind when I had to take care of y'all, but I'm getting older and I'm tired. When I get Rhyann and Phillip out of school, it's gonna be my time. *Time for me.*"

We hear Chester and Phillip when they come through the front door.

Chester heads straight to the kitchen. "Drunken chicken . . . man, I'm starving."

"Make sure you boys clean up the kitchen when you're done. We girls are done for the evening."

We find a chick flick on television and make ourselves comfortable.

Auntie Mo is trying to hide it, but I can tell that she's still bothered by those cheap employers of hers. I hope she tells them off tomorrow. African Americans have been through too much in the past, and it's time we get some respect. If a person does a good job, they should be paid for it, no matter whether their skin color is light or dark.

Chapter 7

can't wait for school to end," Mimi moans when I
catch up with her on Monday morning. "I'm tired of
all this homework and studying." Playing with her ponytail,
she adds, "I'm *sooo* ready for summer vacation. Can you believe it? We still have six more weeks left of school. It might
as well be forever. Ugh."

I agree. "Dee and Alyssa will be out here June sixteenth.
We're gonna have so much fun shopping, hanging out at the
movies, going to the beach, and whatever else we feel like
doing."

At the mention of Divine's upcoming visit, Mimi sighs. "I

wish Dee would just move back to Cali. I still can't believe she actually likes living in that small town. She can visit Alyssa during the summer, but she belongs here with us."

"She's not coming back, Mimi," I tell her. "Not for school anyway, so just get over it. Her mom is living in Atlanta, re-member?" I'm getting irritated with Mimi's constant whining about Divine living in Georgia.

"Well, they still have their house out here, so they might change their minds," she points out. "We have several homes, but this is our main residence. The only reason she was staying there was to be with Madison. That relationship is dead."

"She has T. J. now," I remind her. "They're getting close."

"It won't last."

Her negativity surprises me. "Mimi, why would you say something like that?"

"Divine is a diva. That little preacher's boy is not going to know how to deal with her."

"Have you shared this particular thought with Dee?" I inquire. I know she hasn't, because she and Divine would definitely be on the outs.

"Not really. You know how Dee can be. She'll be ready to move me down to the bottom of her B.F.F. list."

I switch my backpack from one side to the other. "You'd be the same way if she said something like that to you."

"I'm not losing my best friend over some stupid boy."

The bell rings, letting us know that it's time for first period.

Mimi and I have English lit together, so we walk to our class. "By the way, you and Kyle looked pretty cozy at the prom," I say. "What's up with that?"

"He asked me to go with him," she announces with this big stupid grin on her face. "Finally, after a year of trying to get his attention, he asks me to prom. I feel like I've been chasing him forever."

Frowning, I ask, "And you're proud of that?"

Mimi giggles. "It might sound crazy to you, but I really like him, Rhyann."

"Wait till you tell Dee," I say. "She's gonna be so happy for you. She has been saying all along that you two belonged together."

"I know," Mimi responds. "To be honest, I just didn't think it was going to happen. Kyle and Claire have been together since ninth grade. I know he agreed to go with me to the prom, but I wasn't looking for anything more. I just figured he was still in love with Claire."

"That sure didn't last long," I say. "I knew it wouldn't, though. Claire Brett is more into actors, not sons of pro tennis players."

"That's what Dee kept saying. But after the prom, he asked me to be his girlfriend."

"Just be careful," I caution. "Don't rush into anything."

"I already told him that I'd be his girl. Rhyann, c'mon . . . stop the hate for boys, please. There are some really nice ones out there, girl."

"I know that," I respond. "I'm just reminding you of

your own words, Mimi. Go into the relationship just to have fun."

"That's what I'm doing," she says lightly.

Who is this chick trying to kid? Not me, that's for sure.

We head to class bemoaning the fact that we still have another six weeks.

"I'm here, Miss Marilee," I announce when I enter the salon on Tuesday. I came straight from school, excited about paying off my debt. I hate to owe anybody.

"I'm sorry I'm late," I add. "I needed to talk to my history teacher after school, and it took longer than I thought." Mimi's mom drove me here, since she has a hair appointment with Miss Marilee.

"You're fine, dear. I'm glad you were able to make it. How was school?"

I stick my backpack behind the reception desk. "It was okay." Glancing around, I ask, "Where do you want me to start?"

Before Miss Marilee can respond, a skinny woman with flaming red hair, tight designer jeans, and red stiletto heels bursts through the entrance. "Can you believe it? I just got a ticket for jaywalking," she complains. "I told the policeman that I was Samuel Goldberg's wife. He still gave me the ticket."

I glance over at Miss Marilee and then back at the client with the blinging jewelry. *Who is this lady?* I want to ask. *And who is Samuel Goldberg and why should anyone care?*

"He showed me no respect, Marilee. *Not an ounce.*"

The red baron is still complaining when I leave Miss Marilee's side to take some hair products to China. I make a mental note to Google this Samuel Goldberg.

I escort Mimi's mom to the shampoo bowl to wash her hair. Like Mimi, she wears a weave.

"Miss Dean, can I ask you a question?"

"Sure, Rhyann. What is it?"

"How did you get the nickname Dean?" Her name is really Deianira, which I think is really pretty, but everybody calls her Dean.

"When I was born, my brother couldn't pronounce my name, so he just called me Dean. It stuck, and I've been called that ever since."

"Where's that girl?" I hear the red baron ask. I glance around, trying to figure out who she's talking about.

"Marilee, don't you have a new girl working for you?"

"Yes," Miss Marilee says. "Her name is Rhyann."

"Why is she asking about me?" I mumble.

"Did you say something, Rhyann?" Miss Dean asks.

"No, ma'am. Just talking out loud," I respond as I rinse the shampoo out of her hair. I give it one more thorough washing before applying conditioner and setting her under a dryer per Miss Marilee's instructions.

The red baron struts over to me and has the nerve to say, "I'd like a latte and, oh, some of Marilee's delicious lemon cake."

My hands on my hips, I look at her as if she's lost her mind. I guess the word "please" is not in her vocabulary. I hope she knows that I'm not her maid.

She scans me from head to toe. "Pretty girls should always wear a smile. Especially if you're dealing with clients."

"My name is Rhyann."

"It's nice to meet you," she says. "Now would you please get me that latte and a slice of cake? Marilee knows how much I adore her treats."

Whatever.

My gaze travels to Miss Marilee, who gives me a slight nod. I guess it is part of my job to cater to ungrateful Jewish women. Well, at least I'll be done by the end of the week.

I bring Mimi's mom back over to the shampoo bowl and rinse her out. Once I have her in Miss Marilee's chair, it's time for the red baron to get her hair washed.

I give that bright red hair a good washing and send her off to Miss Marilee, but the red baron doesn't tip me a penny.

Talk about a cheapskate.

"How was your first day at work?" my aunt asks when I enter the house four hours later.

"It was fine until the red baron came into the salon," I answer, dropping my fake Gucci purse on the living room sofa. "I'm not a racist or anything, Auntie Mo, but I can't really say the same for her. She kept calling me girl, even after I told her my name several times. And she didn't even leave me a tip. China told me that she never tips anybody, not even Miss Marilee."

"Maybe she is hard of hearing," Auntie Mo suggests.

I shake my head no. "I'm pretty sure she knew my name. I heard her asking Miss Marilee about me, and then I told her my name again. She's nothing but an old cheap Jew."

"Rhyann!" she cries. "Sweetheart, I don't ever want to hear that come out of your mouth again."

"Well, it's the truth."

"It's not a nice thing to say."

"I've heard you say it, Auntie Mo. Maybe not in those words, but the meaning is the same. Just yesterday you came home talking about how cheap Mr. Cohen is."

She's silent for a moment, catching herself. "Then I was at fault. I was a little upset over having to work the dinner party tonight. It doesn't matter, though, because we should never say things like that, Rhyann. It's hurtful and it's wrong."

"They say mean things about us all the time."

"But we don't have to do wrong for wrong, do we?" Auntie Mo asks.

I lower my head. "No, ma'am."

"Chances are, you won't see her again, since you're only working there this week to pay off your bill. Go to the salon and be nice, Rhyann. You can do that for the next few days, right?"

"Yes, ma'am."

I stop by my brothers' room to check Phillip's homework.

Auntie Mo says she doesn't understand all this new math, so I usually help him with this subject. I check his other homework, too.

After I finish, I'm not happy. "You know you can do a better job than this," I say. "Phillip, you need to rewrite your book report."

"Auntie Mo said it was fine."

"It's not bad, but I know you can do a much better job. Some of this is redundant. Just go back over it one more time. Always do your best—that's what Mommy always used to say."

"If I make the corrections, will you type it up for me?" he asks with a hopeful expression.

"It was supposed to be typed?"

"The teacher said we'd get five extra points if we typed it," Phillip replies. "I didn't do it because Brady was on the computer all evening."

I fold my arms across my chest. "Why didn't you go into my room and get on my computer?"

"I tried to call you and ask, but you didn't answer your phone."

Finally I give in. "I'll type it this time, but Phillip . . . don't be trying to play me. You know you could've used my computer for homework."

He gives me a hug. "Thanks, sis."

"This is the last time, Phillip. *I mean it.*"

"Okay."

After my bath, I get on my computer and log onto my

online journal to write something that's been in my head for a couple of days now. One of my favorite things to do is writing poetry. Writing always makes me feel better.

May 5th

My first day at the Crowning Glory Hair Salon went okay except for the redheaded Jewish woman that came in. She got on my nerves big time, but after this week I won't have to see her ever again. Miss Marilee is real nice and so is her daughter, China, who is pregnant. I heard one of the other hairstylists say she's trying to deliver the baby in the salon. She's due tomorrow and still working. I hope she waits until I'm not working there— I don't do babies.

Here is something I've been playing around with and need to put it down so I won't forget it.

*She sits alone for hours on end, thinking about where she went
    wrong
I don't know where I belong
Am I to blame?
Oh what a crying shame*

*She stares in the mirror and wonders if she's pretty enough
Did I have a zit? Am I too thin? Or am I just too tough?
All she wants is a chance
To travel the road to romance*

It would be nice to date the boy she knows so well
But then it might turn into relationship hell
So she decides that it's better to remain friends even though
  heartstrings tug

At the sight of his smile, his laughter and even his shrug
No happy ending here
All because it's a broken heart I fear.

I read over what I've typed so far. I don't have a title for it yet, so I save it as untitled14. My titles don't always come to me when I write my poems.

I write a couple of entries in my journal before getting off the computer. *NCIS* is about to come on, and I do my best to never miss an episode. I love that show.

I'm playing around with the idea of studying forensics, but I'm not totally sold on the idea yet.

Life can be such a challenge sometimes. I'm too young to live alone and stuff, but I'm supposed to know what I want to study in college or what I want to do as a career—which, by the way, has changed so many times over the years.

I'm smart and I'm not ashamed to admit it. I've made straight As for the past six or seven years. I work hard in school because I want to get as far away from the Jungle as possible. It would be a welcome change not to have the sound of helicopters, gunshots, or police sirens lulling me to sleep at night.

Chapter 8

$\mathcal{T}$hankfully, the rest of the week goes off without a hitch.

"Miss Marilee, I want to say thanks for letting me work off my bill," I tell her on Friday. "I've been thinking that if you still need me, I'd like to stay on. If you can't afford to pay me, it's okay, because I'd be happy just getting my tips and getting my hair done every weekend. I can even work on Saturdays if you need me. That's much better than my trying to make money stuffing envelopes. That's such a scam."

"Rhyann, how about I pay you minimum wage plus tips and you still get your hair done weekly?" Miss Marilee counters with a smile. "However, working here can't interfere with your schoolwork, and I'm going to call your aunt just to be sure it's okay with her."

I hug her. "Thanks so much, Miss Marilee. Auntie Mo isn't gonna mind me working part-time as long as I keep my grades up."

"Did you really stuff envelopes?" she asks.

"Yes. I sure did. I was trying to make extra money because I want to go to college. I even have an online business selling greeting cards and stuff, but I'm not making a lot of money."

"You're quite the entrepreneur. That's wonderful."

I run my fingers through my curls. "My aunt's done a lot for me and my brothers and sister. I don't want to depend on her forever, so I have to do something to help myself."

"I'm thrilled to have you on board, Rhyann."

That makes me feel great. Miss Marilee is so nice. "I really appreciate you giving me a chance. This is my first real job, and I promise not to let you down."

"You can fill out the necessary paperwork when you come in on Tuesday."

Chester is outside waiting for me in his car.

"Miss Marilee gave me the job permanently," I announce when I settle down in the front passenger seat. "I have a job."

"Good for you," he says, pleased. "I'm proud of you."

"I'm planning on saving my paycheck and living off my tips and the allowance Auntie Mo gives me."

"I like that. You're being smart." He jabs his thumb behind

him. "You need to teach that to your brother. Brady spends his money as soon as he gets it."

"He'll learn when he's tired of being broke. I don't like not having money."

"Me neither," Chester chimes in.

When I walk into the house, I ask Auntie Mo, "Did Miss Marilee call you?"

"She did," my aunt responds. "She told me that she gave you a job." She looks at me hard. "Is this something you want to do? You know you're gonna have to be nice to the customers even if they work your nerves."

"I'll do what I have to do," I say. "I like making the extra money. My allowance isn't getting it, and neither is my on-line business."

Auntie Mo opens the oven to check on her meat loaf. "Well, as long as it don't interfere with school, then it's fine with me."

I knew she wouldn't have a problem with me working. I'm so excited! I have a job.

"Guess what?" I say to Brady when he arrives home fifteen minutes later. "I'm working at the salon permanently."

"That's good. Will you get a discount when you get your hair done?"

"I get it done for free," I respond. "I'm gonna keep a fresh look."

He chuckles. "Congratulations, sis. I'm glad you're gonna be able to keep that head of yours straight. Some days you can scare a person."

"Funny," I fire back. "Speaking of hair, you need to get something done to your locks. They're looking kind of raggedy."

"I see you had your daily dose of hateration."

Laughing, I head to my room to work on my homework.

I'll be attending a movie premiere with Mimi and her family in a couple of hours. Afterward, I'm spending the weekend with them. I enjoy staying in her huge mansion, but I have to be honest. I'm always happy when it's time to head back to my house.

Mimi's parents are nice, but I'm always feeling like they're putting on an act. When they don't think anybody's paying attention, they completely ignore each other. I'd never mention it to Mimi because she'd have a meltdown. She likes to pretend that her world is perfect.

Divine has noticed it, too, but like me, she is hesitant to say anything to Mimi, especially since we really don't know what's going on. Divine says all the signs of a bad marriage are there. She should know. She survived her parents' breakup and divorce.

"What are you wearing to the premiere?" Mimi inquires while we're hanging out in her gigantic bedroom. My whole house could fit in this room.

"I bought a pair of jeans and this shirt." I hold up a black-and-yellow top I purchased last weekend from Old Navy.

"Why don't you wear one of my shirts?" Mimi suggests. "I have the perfect top for those jeans."

I don't like wearing other people's clothes, so I shake my

head no. "I'm fine with what I brought, Mimi." I don't know why she's always trying to dress me in her stuff whenever we go places.

My clothes may not have somebody else's name on them, but they're still fierce. Humph! I wouldn't be caught dead in some of that mess she wears. Auntie Mo can throw down with a sewing machine. What she doesn't make, I buy from Old Navy. It's one of my favorite places to shop.

Mimi picks up my shirt and eyes it with disgust. "You're sure you don't want to wear one of mine? At leas—"

I interrupt her. "Why are you always trying to get me in your clothes, Mimi? I've told you before—I don't like wearing other people's stuff. I have my own and I like the way I look in them. If you don't think my clothes are nice enough for the premiere . . . well, I can just go home."

She instantly backs down. "Rhyann, don't trip. I was only trying to be nice. I don't shop at Old Navy, but I know that they have nice things. I love some of your outfits."

"You can be such a snob sometimes."

She gives me this wounded look. "I can't help it if I like the better things in life. It's all I know."

"That's what happens when you're born with a Louis Vuitton attached to your hand."

I can tell from Mimi's tight-mouthed expression that she's a little hot with me right now. She's walking around the room looking all flustered and sending glares my way. I don't care, though. She knows I'm telling the truth.

The limo arrives forty-five minutes later and we all pile in.

I can't help but notice that while Mimi and I are running our mouths, her parents haven't said one word to each other. In fact, I think her father is pretending to be asleep.

Upon our arrival, we're pointed toward the red carpet. Mimi's dad is an actor in a very successful television series, so everybody knows who he is. We walk the red carpet as quickly as we can. A couple of photographers lined up along the path snap photos of us as we head to the theater entrance.

Mimi nudges my arm when we step off the red carpet. "Rhyann, look who's here."

I follow Mimi's gaze, my eyes landing on a familiar face.

"Omigosh! What is he doing here?" I wonder aloud. Traven and I haven't talked since the prom. He's called me a couple of times—I just haven't called him back.

"He's stalking you now," Mimi says with a chuckle.

I smile at the thought. "Traven's probably here trying to add another notch to his bedpost. I'm pretty sure he didn't know that I would be here unless Brady mentioned it to him."

"I never figured him for a dog," Mimi whispers.

He glances in our direction and we wave.

"Traven, what are you doing here?" I ask when he walks over. I glance around, checking to see if he came with a female.

"I'm just hanging out with my cousin," he says, pointing to a young man standing a few feet away. "He's been in a couple of music videos and he was an extra in this movie."

"Cool . . . ," I respond.

He glances over at Mimi and smiles. "How you doing?"

"Fine," she responds. "Is Leon your cousin?"

Traven nods. "His dad and my mom are brother and sister."

I laugh. "A simple yes would have been enough, Traven."

Mimi elbows me in the side. "Leave him alone. I know your cousin. He was in a movie with my father a couple of months ago. I met him on the set. He's a good actor."

I look over my shoulder. Mimi's parents are still on the red carpet, talking to the media. Divine loves being on the red carpet, but it's not something Mimi and I care about. I definitely don't want my picture plastered everywhere.

Traven introduces his cousin to me.

"It's nice to meet you, Leon," I say. I recognize him from a couple of music videos. My attention is drawn to a woman making her way down the red carpet.

"Omigosh! Isn't that Dee's stepmom?" I whisper to Mimi. "Ava?" I wonder if she's supposed to be out like this. Divine told me she had doctor's orders to take it easy.

Mimi follows my gaze. "That's her for sure. Wow! Ava looks like she's about to pop that baby out any moment now."

She looks pretty in an aqua maternity dress that comes just above her knees. The white leggings and silver strappy mules she's wearing really complete the look, showing that even though you're pregnant, you can still look fashionable.

"I should take a picture of her and send it to Dee," I say.

Mimi holds out her camera phone and snaps. "Beat you to it."

We acknowledge Ava when she comes toward us.

"You're Divine's friends, right?" Ava asks.

"Yes," Mimi responds. "You know my parents, Richard and Dean Reuben."

Brushing a stray curl out of her face, Ava flashes a pretty smile. "I sure do. I did a feature on your father about three years ago." I know Divine isn't really crazy about her, but she seems nice. It wasn't cool what she did to Miss Kara, but I think she really wants to get to know Divine. Ava was so in love with Jerome that she picked a public fight with Miss Kara and then sued her. Divine said her mom had to pay out a cool million.

I introduce Traven and Leon to Ava. "Leon has a part in the movie."

"Congratulations," she tells him.

Traven and Leon excuse themselves to meet some other family members just arriving.

Ava looks as if she's searching for something to say. She finally settles on, "When you talk to Divine, please tell her that I said hello. Her father told me that she's coming out here in June."

"She is," Mimi confirms. "She and Alyssa will be here June sixteenth."

"Well, I hope to see her during her visit."

"We'll let her know that we saw you," Mimi and I say in unison.

Rubbing her swollen belly, Ava walks over to where Mimi's parents are standing.

"She is really huge," Mimi blurts.

"Yeah," I say. "She kind of looks a bit deformed with her belly being so big. I'm sure she can't wait to get that baby out of her."

Inside the theater, Mimi and I sit with Traven and his family.

Afterward, Traven whispers in my ear, "So what did you really think of the movie?"

I laugh before responding, "It's just okay. What did you think of it?"

He agrees. "I was hoping this would be Leon's big break, but nobody's gonna really notice him. He said that most of the scenes with him in them ended up on the cutting room floor."

"That sucks."

"Yeah," Traven affirms. "Leon's not gonna give up, though. He'll keep auditioning until he makes the big time. That's how he is."

"That's good. He shouldn't give up on his dream."

"He's not," he responds. "It's not in his makeup." His eyes never leave my face.

"Traven, will you stop staring at me like that?" I say in a loud whisper.

"I can't help it. You look so good in that outfit."

"It's just a pair of jeans and a shirt, Traven." This dude is so full of it.

"You look great in everything. Well, except that ugly plaid skirt you have to wear to school."

I laugh. "What are you talking about, Traven? Humph! I look good in navy-and-green plaid."

We walk toward the nearest exit door, merging with the sea of people who came to the premiere.

Leon gestures for Traven to join him, so I look for Mimi, who's a few yards away. I wait for her to catch up. "What happened to you?"

"I saw Bow Wow and went over to say hello."

"Girl, you should've told me," I say. "I love me some Bow Wow."

"I figured you'd sworn off boys, and besides, you were over there talking to Traven."

"Humph. If I'd known you were going to talk to Bow Wow, I would've left him in the dust."

Mimi's parents usher us into the limo so that we can head to a reception being held at a nearby hotel.

I look for Traven as soon as we arrive but don't see him.

"They haven't arrived yet," Mimi tells me. "Don't worry. Traven should be here soon."

I send her a sharp glare. "I told you that he's just like the other guys. All he thinks about is sex."

"You two just seemed so happy at the prom," Mimi says when she walks up to the buffet table. "I thought that maybe Traven was going to be your boyfriend."

"We're friends." I fill Mimi in on what Traven said prom night. "Now do you understand why I'm keeping my distance? He figured we'd get it on in the limo—how tacky is that?"

"Rhyann, it's just you and me. Why won't you admit you like the boy?" Mimi asks, folding her arms across her chest. "It's like, so obvious."

I feel the hair on the back of my neck stand up, and I glance over my shoulder. Traven is coming into the room, as if on cue.

"Mimi, will you keep your voice down? He's right over there," I say. "I'll be honest. I was interested in dating him, but not anymore."

She peeks behind me. "Rhyann, are you sure?"

"Traven is a playa. Mimi, I deserve better."

I pick up a glass containing six shrimp and some cocktail sauce, then, using the utensils provided, I grab two mini crab cakes and place them on my plate. We head to the jalapeño meatballs next.

"Rhyann, I know you have feelings for Traven. And he seems crazy about you."

I shrug. "Doesn't matter."

"So you won't give him a chance?"

"I can't. Mimi, when Traven was having girlfriend issues, he came to me for advice. When I was having boy problems, Traven was there for me. Who do we go to if we're the ones involved?" I release a long sigh. "I don't know. Maybe I am scared because I don't want to risk losing a friend. He's really been there for me, you know? Almost like a big brother. I know all his secrets, and that boy loves himself some girls. He already told me that he's cheated on two of his ex-girlfriends. I don't need all that drama in my life."

During the past year, my feelings for Traven began to transform slowly, but I'm not about to open my heart for him to trample all over it.

I follow Mimi over to the table where her mother is sitting. It might be my imagination, but to me, Miss Dean doesn't look too happy being left alone at the table like that. Her mouth is clenched tight, and she looks unapproachable.

"Maybe we should give your mom some space," I whisper to Mimi.

"Why? She's just sitting here by herself. We should keep her company." Mimi drops down in the empty chair next to her mother and asks, "Where's Father?"

"He's making the rounds," her mother responds dryly. "Mimi dear, you're old enough to know the game."

One of the waiters working the reception brings over a plate of food for her. "Your husband asked that I deliver this to you," he says. "He wasn't sure what you wanted to drink, though."

"I'll take a glass of white wine, please."

"That's so sweet of Father," Mimi says with a smile.

Her mother does not respond.

Traven and Leon stroll over to the table, and Mimi quickly invites them to join us. My personal matchmaker. Thankfully, Leon doesn't ask our opinion of the movie.

The waiter returns with Miss Dean's wine. She downs it quickly and asks for another. I pretend not to notice.

I spend the rest of my evening talking and dancing with Traven. Kyle and his father show up around midnight after coming from another function. Mimi practically jumps in Kyle's arms, she's so happy to see him. Leon takes turns dancing with me and Mimi.

"Your cousin is so nice," I tell Traven. "I like him."

"We're very close."

"I can tell. You two act more like brothers than you and Todd."

"Me and Todd, we're close, too."

"But you seem more like best friends to me."

"That's because we are," he says. "Todd is my best friend."

I guess Miss Dean has had enough of sitting at the table alone, so she walks out to the dance floor to announce that we're leaving in a couple of minutes. I spot Mimi's dad standing a few yards away talking to some woman who looks at least twenty years younger than him. Mimi's mom sees him at about the same time and heads straight for them.

The woman makes a quick disappearing act while Miss Dean looks like she's giving her husband an earful.

"Mother's sure in a mood," Mimi whispers when we spot her coming back to the table. "She's going to want to leave. I bet she's got another one of her headaches."

I can't tell if Mimi is covering for her mother or she actually believes what she's saying. I rise to my feet when she says, "We'd better get going."

We say our good-byes and head to the nearest exit.

This is exactly what I'm trying to avoid. Getting played is so out of fashion this season.

Chapter 9

The next morning, Mimi's parents allow us to sleep until ten, which I truly appreciate. Auntie Mo would be like, *"Time to get up. It's almost eight o'clock and you need to get your chores out of the way. The day will be gone before you know it."*

Like, where's it going?

Mimi's parents have a housekeeper, so they don't do any of the cleaning or laundry. Mimi gets an allowance that's twice what I get and she doesn't do a thing to earn it. I'm not hating on her, though. I don't mind working for my money.

Mimi's my friend and all, but she's a spoiled brat and she knows it.

Divine calls the house around noon to talk to Mimi. I pick up one of the extensions so that I can join the conversation.

Divine asks, "So who went to the premiere last night besides Ava? Anything happen that I should know about?"

Divine likes to stay up on all the Hollywood gossip.

"Nobody special was there," Mimi responds. "Oh, Traven was there with his cousin Leon. You know him—Leon's been a dancer in Usher's music video, and he was in one of Omarion's videos, too."

"He was also in *The Father's Day Project* with your dad, too," I interject.

"Yeah, he was."

"I think I know who you're talking about. He's the one with the cross tattooed on his shoulder, right?"

"Yeah," I respond. "He's really trying to break into acting."

We talk a little more about him until the conversation changes to fashion.

"My mom bought these cute shoes from Bloomingdale's," Divine tells us. "I can't wait to come to Los Angeles, because I want to see if I can find some more. They come in red, black, and navy. I want to get the red ones."

"I bought some fierce sandals from T.J. Maxx," I announce, not to be outdone. "They only cost me twenty-nine dollars, and I'm telling you . . . they are so cute."

"I didn't know that T.J. Maxx sold shoes," Mimi says.

"Mimi, have you ever been in a T.J. Maxx store?" Dee inquires with a chuckle.

"I think I have," she responds. "Didn't I go with you one time, Rhyann?"

"If you did, I don't remember."

"Girl, we went to T.J. Maxx when you wanted to pick out a Christmas present for Chester, remember?"

"Oh, yeah."

"It had some nice stuff, but you kind of have to really look for it," Mimi says doubtfully. "Too much work."

She is sounding defensive, and Divine picks up on it. Smooth as silk, she changes the subject. "I can't believe Ava is so huge," Divine says. "If you hadn't sent me that picture, I wouldn't have believed it."

"Dee, are you still planning on spending time with her when you come out here?" Mimi questions.

"I promised Jerome that I would. I'm spending like a week with her after the baby is born. I want to get to know my baby sister—that's the only reason."

Divine is still a little upset over Jerome and Ava getting married, although she denies it. Deep down, she really would like her parents back together. She's also not too thrilled that her mom is engaged to that fine Kevin Nash. I wish Auntie Mo could find a man like that. I certainly wouldn't have a problem with it at all.

"How does your mom feel about you spending time with Ava?" Mimi asks.

"She says that it won't bother her. She's too into Kevin and planning their wedding right now."

"You can't blame her," I interject. "Your mom is getting

married. She's excited. You know we'd be feeling the same way if it was us."

"You're right," Mimi says. "I just know that she doesn't like Ava."

"Mom's not tripping off her anymore," Divine states. "She and Jerome are cool with each other. I guess they're trying to be friends or something for my sake," she says, sounding annoyed. "It beats having all the divorced parent drama."

"I'm so glad my parents are happy with each other," Mimi states. "I'm so lucky."

Divine and I both remain silent, not wanting to burst her little bubble. Mimi's parents don't even look like they're together when they are standing side by side. If they're a happy couple, I would rather have misery for the rest of my life, because they look like they can barely stand to be in the same room together. He even left her sitting at a table alone for most of the evening.

I know Mimi's very self-absorbed, but c'mon . . . can she really be that blind?

May 12th

I had so much fun at the movie premiere on Saturday. I think it was mostly because Traven was there. Mimi is cool and one of my best friends, but she can be so self-centered at times, it can be a little frustrating. I spent the weekend with Mimi and her family. Now it's Monday and back to another week of school. At least I have my new job, which I start officially tomorrow.

It's time for me to leave for school, so I have to end this entry for now. I'll write more soon.

As soon as I step on campus, I walk over to the area where Mimi and I hang out every morning until the bell rings. She's already there.

Her face is red and her eyes are swollen.

"What's wrong?" I ask. "Did something happen?"

"Kyle and I had a fight."

I sit down beside her, dropping my backpack on the ground. "About what, Mimi?"

"That's just it. I don't really know. He just started tripping on me." A single tear rolls down her cheek.

"Mimi, don't cry," I say. "Get yourself together, girl. You don't want Kyle to see you sitting over here crying like a baby."

She pulls a tissue out of her purse and wipes her face.

"Now touch up your makeup. You never let a boy see you cry. What in the world are you thinking? You're about to lose your cool points with me."

Mimi repairs her makeup and then asks, "Okay, how do I look?"

I smile. "Like a diva."

"I'm crazy about Kyle, but I don't know if I can handle those stupid moods of his."

I don't like the sound of that. "You better check that dude. Don't get so wrapped up with him that you need to go into therapy or something."

She chuckles. "I'm not going out like that. I just get so frustrated because I don't know what I keep doing wrong."

"It's probably him, Mimi. Kyle has issues—that's what it sounds like."

I dispense more relationship advice until the bell rings, as if I'm Doctor Love.

I haven't taken two steps before this girl nearly runs me over trying to catch up with her friends. I break into a run to catch up with her with Mimi hot on my tracks.

I reach out and grab the girl by the arm before Mimi can stop me. This is another Jewish person acting like they have the right to walk over people. "Hey! It's only polite to say excuse me when you almost knock a person down."

"What are you talking about?" she responds, snatching her arm away.

"You practically knocked me down back there."

"No, I didn't," she argues.

I take a step forward, invading her space. "Yeah, you did, and I don't appreciate it. You better stop being so rude before somebody gives you a beat down."

I walk off. Normally, I don't fly off the handle like that, but I'm tired of the way my family is treated by Jewish people. The Cohens are giving my aunt a hard time since she demanded more money, and now this chick is trying to walk through me as if I'm invisible. I really can't stand Jews right now.

This is not the way I wanted my day to begin.

By lunchtime, Mimi and Kyle are back on speaking terms.

I'm trying to eat lunch and he's hugging and kissing on her like they're the only two people sitting here.

"Maybe you two should get a room," I say dryly.

Mimi laughs. "Kyle's leaving school early today. He has a doctor's appointment."

Like I care.

I try to finish off my sub sandwich without getting sick to my stomach from the two lovebirds.

Finally, I've had enough and I say, "I'll see you later. Bye, Kyle."

He hands me my backpack and returns his attention to Mimi.

Seeing them together like this only reminds me of how lonely I feel at times. Plus, I'm a little irritated that Kyle intruded during the time Mimi and I have together. The lunch period is our time. At least that's the way it's supposed to be.

The rest of the school day drags by slowly.

By the time I reach my sixth-period class, I'm so ready for the bell to ring. Today just wasn't a good day at all.

My Tuesday starts much better.

After school, I take the bus to the salon. Auntie Mo has to work late again, so I'll see her at home later. When she called me, I could tell she was upset. She even said something about quitting.

The red baron blows into the salon with her red hair and

red nails. This time she's wearing a crisp white linen pantsuit with a red patent leather belt. I like her red patent leather sandals, too, with the matching handbag.

"Is that little girlie here today?" Ann Goldberg asks as soon as she's seated in Miss Marilee's chair. "Oh, there you are. I'll take a latte and some lemon pound cake."

"Please . . ." First I had to deal with Gilda nearly knocking me down yesterday and now her. *What is it with these people?*

"Excuse me," the red baron says. "Did you say something?"

I turn around, my hands on my hips. "Yeah, I did," I snap. "I have a name, and it's definitely not '*girl*' or '*girlie.*' It would be nice if you'd say please every now and then. Just in case you didn't get the memo, slavery ended years ago, so I don't have to be your handmaid. I'm not gonna let some white woman talk to me any kind of way. Sorry, but I'm not having it."

The red baron's mouth drops wide open.

"Rhyann, can I speak to you in the office?" Miss Marilee asks, but from the expression on her face, I can tell it's not a request but a demand.

She closes the door behind me.

"I think it would be best for you to go home today."

"Miss Marilee, I won't stand to be disrespected," I say. "She's very rude."

"In order to get respect, one must earn respect, Rhyann. Just go on home and we'll talk tomorrow."

"But—"

Miss Marilee repeats, "It's best if you go on home. As I said, we'll talk tomorrow. I want you to really think about what it means to work here."

I grab my backpack and leave.

On the way out, I hear someone tell Miss Marilee that China's husband just called to say that she's in labor and on her way to the hospital. He wants her to bring the baby clothes to the hospital because he forgot them.

"I'll drive you home," she tells me. "I need to go by China's place to pick up some things."

In the car, Miss Marilee isn't real talkative. I don't know if it's because she's mad at me or worried about her daughter.

"I'm sorry," I say softly.

"I know that, Rhyann. But I don't want you to be sorry. I want you to decide if you really want this job."

I keep my mouth shut during the rest of the ride home.

I make a pot of spaghetti so Auntie Mo won't have to come home and cook, then I start my homework and work until she arrives.

"Do you think I'll get fired?" I ask Auntie Mo, after telling her what happened.

"Not if you apologize, Rhyann. Not just to Marilee but to the client as well."

"But—" I begin.

Auntie Mo cuts me off. "But nothing. Rhyann, listen to me. If you want to keep your job, then you need to let what people say just roll down your back. Do your job—that's all that matters."

"I can't let people talk to me any kind of way, Auntie Mo."

"You are a child, Rhyann. If someone gives you a problem, tell your employer about it and let her handle it. Isn't that what I tell you about your teachers?"

I'm still mad, and I don't respond.

"Did you hear me?"

"Yes, ma'am."

"Rhyann, if you want this job, then you need to do the right thing. You can't go around flying off the handle just because you think you're bad. All that happens is that you end up unemployed. You have to learn to choose your battles wisely."

Then she embraces me. "Thanks so much for cooking dinner, sweetie. I appreciate it."

"You're welcome," I murmur.

It's Brady's night to do the dishes, so I head to my bedroom right after dinner. I log onto my journal.

May 13th

Today I told off the red baron, and I think Miss Marilee is going to fire me for doing so. I just got tired of being called "girl" or "girlie." I have a name and I would like people to use it when referring to me. What's so wrong with that?

My aunt says I have to choose my battles wisely. So when am I supposed to fight? Over the years, we fought for freedom; we fought for the right to vote; we fight even now for respect.

Although people try to deny it, racism still lives. So am I not supposed to demand the respect I deserve?

Miss Marilee said that in order to get respect, I have to earn it—what is she talking about?

Why should I let some white woman call me anything but my name?

Chapter 10

I didn't sleep well, so I wake up Wednesday morning a little cranky. Plus, Auntie Mo's car has a flat, and we have to wait for Chester to fix it, which makes me late for school and her late for work.

I can see how this day is going to turn out already.

When I finally get to school, first period has already started. There's only about thirty minutes left.

When the bell rings for second period, I make a quick stop by my locker. Thank goodness this is PE. I need something to wake me out of my funk.

Mimi walks up to me. "Hey, what happened this morning? Why were you so late?"

"Car trouble. Auntie Mo had a flat tire."

"Oh."

Kyle strolls over to where we're standing. "I was just looking for you," he tells Mimi.

I'm not in the mood for him draping himself all over her, so I excuse myself. "Mimi, I'll see you at lunch."

"Okay."

Lunch isn't for another two periods, so I grab a bag of crackers out of my backpack and nibble on them on my way to my third-period Latin class. Once there, we find out that we're having a pop quiz.

Great.

Normally this doesn't bother me, but the way my week has been going, I just might fail the test.

We have to translate a series of sentences into idiomatic Latin. I read the first one: "They kept asserting that the sailors would be killed."

I pick up my pen and write *Affirmabant nautas necatum iri.* Satisfied, I move on to the next one. Thankfully, there are only four of them, and I'm pretty sure I have the correct answers.

The crackers I scarfed down earlier on my way to class do nothing to keep my hunger at bay. I'm starving by the time fourth period ends, so I head straight to the cafeteria.

I already have my sandwich by the time Mimi arrives.

She sets her tray of food down on the table. "Rhyann, what's up? Why are you so quiet?"

"I'm stressed, Mimi," I respond. "I'm worried that Miss

Marilee is gonna fire me over that white woman. I didn't mean to cause drama, but you know I can't stand it when people try to act like they so much better than me. That woman was treating me like I was a house slave or something, so I got in her face."

Much of my problem is that I've been fretting over being fired all last night and this morning. I really enjoy working at the Crowning Glory Hair Salon and don't want to lose my job. I reach for the bottle of ketchup and pour some over my french fries.

"I would've told her off, too," Mimi says before biting into her chicken wrap sandwich. After chewing and swallowing, she adds, "I'm with you on that."

"I probably should've just gone and told Miss Marilee so she could handle it. That's what my aunt said anyway. She knows my temper. I'm gonna apologize to her this afternoon."

"Miss Marilee's nice. I don't think she's going to fire you, Rhyann. I'm pretty sure she'll give you another chance. It's not like you beat up the red baron." She giggles. "Now you got me calling her that."

I laugh. "That's the perfect nickname for her. You should see that fire engine red hair. I can't lie, though. It looks good on her."

I stick a french fry into my mouth.

"Your hair really looks cute, Rhyann."

Giving Mimi a sidelong glance, I respond, "Thanks. I'm getting used to it like this, but I plan on letting it grow out again. I'm gonna get braids for the summer."

"Well, you already know that you look good with braids, too." Mimi finishes off her sandwich. She takes a long swig of her Pepsi before biting into her apple.

Our conversation turns to Mimi's favorite subject. Kyle.

Mimi finishes her apple. "He's so moody at times. Sometimes I don't know how to deal with him."

This is the second time I'm hearing doubts. "I don't know what's up with Kyle. Maybe he's just not as into you as much as you think."

"Rhyann, don't hate. I can't help it if I'm cute and I'm a boy magnet."

"If I had a dollar sign tattooed on my forehead like you and Dee, I'm sure I'd meet a lot of boys, too." I take a sip of my soda before eating the last of my fries. "But don't think I'm sleeping when it comes to a boy. *I get lots of attention.* I'm just extremely picky about the ones I let up in my life."

Mimi leans forward and says in a loud whisper, "Rhyann, please, I need you to help me figure out how to make Kyle happy."

I survey her face to see if she's serious. "What do you mean by that?"

"He can be so nice to me some days, and then others, he acts like he doesn't want to be bothered. What am I doing wrong?"

"Are you always calling him?" I ask. "Boys don't like girls who are always so needy."

"I have a life," Mimi says, offended. "I don't call him every day or anything like that."

I shrug. "So just back off some more and see what happens."

"But I don't want Kyle to think that I'm not interested in him."

I chuckle. "He won't think that. Not the way you chased after him like that."

The bell rings a few minutes later.

"I'll be so glad to get this day over with," I say.

When school lets out, I walk down to the bus stop to catch the bus to the salon. I pray the whole way there that I'll still have a job.

As soon as I arrive, I find out that China has given birth to a little girl. I make a mental note to buy a gift for the baby.

I locate Miss Marilee in her office. I knock before walking in.

"Have a seat, Rhyann," she says.

I remain standing. "Miss Marilee, please don't fire me," I plead. "I'm so sorry for going off on the red . . . I mean, Mrs. Goldberg, like that. I was wrong, and I'm truly sorry."

Miss Marilee looks at me severely. "Rhyann, we pride ourselves on providing excellent customer service even to our more difficult clients. Ann Goldberg is brisk, and she says whatever comes into her head, but I've known her a long time and I can tell you that she doesn't mean any harm. It takes her some time to learn names. If it wasn't for that BlackBerry she carries everywhere, she probably wouldn't remember her appointments."

"Oh," I mutter.

"If you're going to work here, I need to know that you can hold your tongue. If any of the clients give you a hard time, just tell me, and I'll handle it. Okay?"

"Yes, ma'am."

She smiles warmly, liking that I know I was wrong. "Then let's not keep the clients waiting. We're going to be pretty busy with China out with the baby."

"Oh, by the way, congratulations, Grandma." I say.

Her smile goes ten watts brighter. "Rhyann, my new granddaughter is the most beautiful baby in the world."

"Do you have pictures of her?" I ask.

"Not yet, but I'm taking some tonight when I go out to Kaiser."

My spirits are lifted now that I know I'm still employed. I send up a quick prayer of thanks. "Oh, Miss Marilee, I forgot to tell you that I have Bible study on Wednesday nights. I need to leave by six."

"Your aunt told me. That's fine."

We leave the office, and I call for the first client to come to the shampoo bowl. By the time I have to go, I've washed twenty heads and made fifty dollars in tips. One client, an actress, tipped me twenty dollars alone. Is it any wonder why I want to keep this job?

I stroll out of the salon expecting to see Chester or Auntie Mo waiting for me, especially since I have to go straight to the church, but I find Traven sitting in his cute little Mustang.

I walk over to his car. "Hey, Traven. What are you doing here?"

Before he can respond, this chick in jeans that are much too tight walks up to the car and plops herself down in the front passenger side without a word to me.

Traven introduces us. She eyes me up and down before plastering on a fake smile and saying hello. I respond in kind.

To Traven, I say, "I'll just wait for my aunt to pick me up."

"She asked me to pick you up," he responds. "C'mon, Rhyann. I told her that I'd drop you off at the church."

The last thing I want to do is ride with him and his chick of the day.

Traven's eyes never leave my face. "I promised her that I'd get you there on time. You see, I called the house earlier to talk to Brady. Your aunt told me that you needed a ride, and she asked if I could pick you up since I was over this way."

He gets out and walks around the car to open the door for me. This dude is putting me in the backseat.

That's okay. I don't mind.

"Thanks for coming all the way over here," I say when I get in. "I'll give you some gas money."

"Keep your money, Rhyann. I'm cool. Besides, I'm down this way a lot. My cousin and his family don't live too far from here." Traven walks back to the driver's side, and soon we're on our way.

He drops his *friend* off two blocks away from the salon.

"You want to get up front?" he has the nerve to ask me.

"No, I'm fine back here," I respond, trying not to show that I have an attitude with him.

"She's just a friend of my cousin's," Traven tries to explain. "I was doing him a favor and giving her a ride."

"You're doing a lot of favors today, huh?" I ask. Deep down, I'm thrilled he's not dating her. I can tell that we wouldn't be able to get along.

He steals a peek over his shoulder at me. "Hey, you okay?"

"I'm good," I respond. He still looks suspicious, so I add, "Did you get your car painted? It looks different."

Traven nods. "Yeah. I just got it back yesterday."

"It looks like a brand-new car," I say. "Looks like you got the inside redone, too."

He laughs. "I just had it cleaned real good."

I settle back against the seat. "I can't wait to get my own car. Chester is looking for a car for Brady. He and Auntie Mo are giving it to him for graduation. It's a surprise, so don't tell him."

"I won't," he promises. "Chester and I went to this dealership in Inglewood to check on this Mustang. It was sweet, but the price was too high."

"So you knew about it then—the car for Brady."

Traven glances over at me. "Only because I was riding with Chester at the time. He was giving me a lift to pick up my car after it got painted."

"Is Chester looking for a car for me, too?" I ask hopefully.

"He didn't mention it to me."

"I hope so. He found one for Tameka, and now he's

looking for one for Brady. I'd better be next on the list."

He glances over the seat at me. "What kind of car do you want? A BMW or Lexus?"

"Nope," I reply. "I want a Volkswagen Beetle convertible. Yellow with the black top."

He thinks that's funny. "I can see you driving one of those."

"Traven, why did you say a BMW or Lexus?" I ask. "Why would you think I'd want one of those?" I know this boy can't think I'm a materialistic slave to all things designer.

"They're nice cars," he answers. "I figured you'd want one or the other. I want a BMW, but I can't afford one, not even one like Chester drives. This Mustang used to be my uncle's car. They passed it on to me when he died."

"It's a nice car."

"Hey—I like it, and it beats walking or taking the bus any day."

"Amen to that," I respond. "That's why I'm trying to get Auntie Mo to buy me a car now instead of waiting until I graduate. That way she doesn't have to drive me to school when she's not working."

He gives me an eye. "It's not that far, Rhyann."

"It's farther than Dorsey. Matter of fact, the school isn't even in Los Angeles. I go to school in Pacific Palisades, and she works in Santa Monica. I feel bad when she has to drive me to school on her days off."

He pulls into the church parking lot.

"So, when are we going out again?" he asks me.

I stop with my hand on the door handle. "Traven, I'm focusing on my education. I'm going to college so I can get away from the Jungle, you know."

This boy has no idea how much I like him, and I don't plan on telling him. This way I won't end up looking all embarrassed.

His mouth quirks, like he knows something's wrong. "If you're worried about our friendship, you don't have to be. Rhyann, we'll always be friends. Even if a relationship between us ends up not working."

I shake my head no. "Don't believe that hype. Traven, when I break up with a boy, I'm not trying to be friends after that. I like to leave the past behind."

"So you're saying that we can't be friends if a relationship doesn't work out?"

"Would you want to be friends with a snake that bit you? I wouldn't. If we break up, it's probably gonna be a bad one."

"Stop being so negative." Traven holds his hand out to me. "Who says that we'll even break up? The feelings I have for you are real, Rhyann."

"Maybe you believe that now," I respond. "But it might change over time."

"Pessimistic much?"

"I'm just being cautious."

"I understand," Traven states. "Rhyann, I'm not playing games with you. I really do care for you. *Believe that.*"

Yeah, right.

"I'm not gonna give up on you. I just want you to know."
We'll see.

Luckily, I see Auntie Mo pull into the parking lot. The adults have Bible study on Wednesdays as well. She gets out of her car and waves.

"I guess I'd better go," I say, then pause for a second before asking, "Want to come in for Bible study?"

"I would, but I need to finish a project for my science class. It's due on Friday. Maybe next Wednesday?"

"Sure," I respond. I'm glad we've had a chance to talk. I've always liked talking to him. "I'll give you a call later on tonight. Thanks for the ride."

Auntie Mo waits for me just inside the sanctuary. "Hey, sweetie. How did it go with Marilee?"

"Great! I still have a job."

"Praise the Lord," she says with a smile. "I really appreciate Traven bringing you to the church for me."

I frown at that statement. "I can't believe you're trying to play matchmaker, Auntie Mo."

"Who, me?"

"Uh-huh . . ." I loop my hand through hers and whisper, "I forgive you, though."

Auntie Mo heads off to a classroom for the women while I join the teens in another class for a study on the Book of Matthew.

Kelly walks up to me before I enter the classroom.

"I heard you were trying out. Why didn't you tell me?" she demands with her hands on her hips.

"Because I wasn't sure if I was gonna do it," I respond, staring her down. I know this chick is not trying to check me. I don't have to answer to her about nothing. "What does it matter?"

She seems a bit taken aback by my attitude, but I don't care. She's not my mama, so I don't report to her.

We walk off to an empty classroom.

"I thought we were friends, Rhyann. You know how much I want this."

"I want to be on the praise team, too," I respond. "I told you that. Besides, it's only an audition. We're not the only ones trying out. We may not even get it."

"I'm not worried about getting the spot, Rhyann. I was just shocked that you'd be trying to get it, too."

"You shouldn't be," I retort. "I wanted to be on the praise team long before you decided to do it."

"Since you've been hanging with your little rich friends, I thought maybe you'd changed your mind."

I decide since I'm on holy ground that I'll ignore her little dig. "My friends have nothing to do with me wanting to be on the Temple of Praise squad. Anyway, I'm going inside before my aunt starts looking for me."

Kelly prances out of the room ahead of me.

I don't know why she's tripping like that. It's not like I've already won the spot, but even if I do get it, then I deserve it. I hadn't totally made up my mind if I was auditioning for sure, but now I'm going for it. Don't nobody try to flip on me like that.

Kelly and I usually sit together during Bible study, but not this time. I sit near the window, while she goes to the other side of the room.

Whatever.

The way I see it, Kelly is the one who's wrong. I wanted to be on the praise team first, and I should be the one auditioning. She just wants this because I want to do it—that's how she is. Kelly is the type of person who wants to be constantly in the spotlight.

Before I received my scholarship to Stony Hills Prep, she and I attended the same school and had some of the same classes. Kelly and I were pretty close until I found out she was taking some of my ideas and claiming them as her own. To others, it looked like I was copying her, but that wasn't the case.

Auntie Mo told me that I needed to just keep my ideas to myself because some people just weren't creative enough to come up with their own stuff. She told me to forgive Kelly and move on.

I did what Auntie Mo told me, but I can't deny that every time I see Kelly, I'm tempted to give her a good ol' beat down because of that stuck-up attitude of hers. If she don't stay out of my way tonight, I just might give in to temptation.

Auntie Mo and I stop to pick up hamburgers and fries for dinner tonight since she's not in the mood for cooking and neither am I. Phillip is with Tameka, so they probably grabbed something to eat already, and Brady is working. Who knows where Chester is—he met some girl on the internet, and they are supposed to be meeting in person either tonight or tomorrow.

After I eat and shower, I spend the rest of my evening writing in my online journal.

May 14th

To My Best Friend

Although I've known you for a very long time,
I still remember that day we first met
You took me by complete surprise
I knew that very moment my heart was set

As years flew by and the more we talked,
You never seemed to care if I had bad hair
Or just being mean for no reason
No matter what, you were always there

The more our friendship grew and grew
I started to realize just how much I cared
But to tell you the truth, this feeling is new
It hit me, what this is all about

A different and precious love
For the person I called friend

It's a *Curl* Thing

Is an angel sent from above
The times I spend with you,
Are what makes my heart complete
One thing for sure I know,
Without you in my life,
My future is obsolete

Chapter 11

*A*h, Rhyann, you're here today," Anne Goldberg says when she walks into the salon for her weekly appointment the Tuesday after Memorial Day.

"I'm here," I reply quietly. I'm definitely not in the mood to see this woman, but I promised Miss Marilee that I wouldn't tell Mrs. Goldberg off, so I'm gonna be cool. I'll just ignore her for the most part. Thankfully, she'll only be here for a few hours. I can deal with her for that long, I suppose.

"I'm so glad you're here," she tells me. "I feel dreadful about what happened, and I want to apologize. I certainly didn't mean to offend you, dear. I never meant to make you feel that we're less than equals. I'm not like that at all."

"It's okay," I respond with a slight shrug. "I'm sorry for tripping. I shouldn't have talked to you like that."

"No, it isn't," she counters. "It's never okay to hurt someone, even when it's unintentional." She suddenly gives me a warm smile. "I noticed the last time I was here that you and I have something in common."

"What's that?" I ask, my eyebrows rising in curiosity.

"We both love toffee-ettes." She holds out a See's black-and-white canister to me. "Please accept these as a token of my sincerity."

Stunned, I respond, "Mrs. Goldberg, you didn't have to do this."

Okay, now I feel smaller than an ant. My aunt's words come back to haunt me. I definitely didn't choose this battle well.

"I want you to have them," she insists.

I grin, because I love the bite-size pieces of rich butter toffee with whole almonds smothered in milk chocolate and covered with bits of toasted almonds. "See's is my favorite candy store. Thank you so much for thinking of me, Mrs. Goldberg."

She and I are totally cool now.

I lead her to the shampoo bowl so that I can get started on her hair. When she's seated, I pull out a plastic cape and place it around her neck, making sure to tuck her shirt collar underneath.

Mrs. Goldberg pulls a photograph from her purse. "I want

to show you something. This is my mother. Do you notice anything about her?"

I note the numbers tattooed on the woman's arm. Stunned, I ask, "Did she . . . live during the Holocaust?"

Mrs. Goldberg nods. "So you see, not only do we share a love for toffee-ettes—we also share a history of oppression, Rhyann. That is your name, right?" She places a hand to her temple. "My memory is terrible at times."

When I nod, she continues. "We both have a history of being discriminated against, prevented from owning land, tortured, and murdered."

While I wash her hair, Mrs. Goldberg shares her family history with me.

"My grandfather's business was taken over and my mother's Jewish school was closed. They were deported to Wester-Faengle, a Nazi concentration camp, before being transferred to Auschwitz. My mother and her sister were selected for forced labor and assigned to work on road repairs. My grandmother had a job sorting through the possessions brought into the camp."

"Wow . . . ," I murmur. "It's not much different than slavery and what my ancestors had to endure. The way the slaves were treated was bad, but the way the Jews were gassed and burned alive like that—"

"It wasn't just the Jews. There were African Americans in the concentration camps, too."

When she tells me that my people were also victimized during the Holocaust, I'm totally in shock.

"I've never heard about any blacks in the Holocaust, Mrs. Goldberg. Are you sure about this?"

"There were," she confirms. "My mother told me about the ones she saw and how cruelly they were treated. Many of the African American soldiers fell in love with German women and had children. Now the Nazis . . . they didn't like the notion of mixed-race children at all. The Gestapo—that was the secret German police—they had a lot of them sterilized; they experimented on some, and many of them just mysteriously disappeared."

"I still can't believe it," I say.

"Have you heard of Valaida Snow? She was a jazz musician. She was in Denmark but ended up arrested and sent to Wester-Faengle."

I shake my head no. I repeat the name over and over in my head, because I intend to Google her. I want to know more about this woman and especially her part in the Holocaust.

"My mother said she used to sing to the children. She met her when they were in Wester-Faengle."

"As if slavery wasn't enough . . . ," I whisper. I'm almost afraid to ask, but I have to find out what happened to her. "Did Valaida Snow live long enough to leave the camp?"

"She did," Miss Goldberg confirms. "She returned to the United States, but from what I understand, she was never the same after that. It's such a shame, because I've listened to some of her music and it's beautiful."

"I can believe that," I say, shuddering at what she went

through. "I'm glad your mother survived that horrible time."

"Yes, she did, but the rest of her family didn't. My grandmother died in Auschwitz. My aunt was gassed a few months later. My mother was liberated in 1945 . . . at least I think it was in forty-five. Anyway, she was liberated during a death march from the Malchow camp, where she'd been transferred. She came to America, where she met and married my father. They had seven children—me being the youngest. They were very happy until my father died last year."

"Whew . . . I'm so glad to hear that she had kind of a happy ending, especially after living through all that."

"My mother told me that there were black troops who came to help liberate the camps. Did you know that? They were witness to some of the worst atrocities." She shakes her head sadly. "I can't even imagine having to live through that time."

I'm still stunned by all that I've learned. "The thing is, I've never heard anything about black troops or blacks in general being connected to the Holocaust. You're the first person I've met who is even related to a survivor. Does your mother have nightmares or anything about those days?"

"She used to but not anymore. She's always been a strong woman. I tell her she's my hero all the time. Her courage and her strength saw her through the horror. I think I would've lost my mind if I'd had to go through something like that."

I nod my head in agreement.

I gently guide her head back so that I can rinse her hair.

"The water's not too hot for you, is it?" I inquire.

"No, it's fine," she responds. "It feels good. I have a lot of headaches, so please be gentle. The last shampoo girl—I can't remember her name—anyhoo, she was much too rough whenever she washed my hair. I'd go home with the worst pain sometimes."

I take special care, not that I wouldn't be gentle anyway.

"You're very good with your hands," Mrs. Goldberg compliments as I prop her up in the chair. "My scalp feels so good. I hope Marilee keeps you around for a long time."

"Thank you," I respond. "I learned how to wash hair from my sister. She's in cosmetology school."

"Where do you go to school?"

"Stony Hills Prep."

Her eyes widen in surprise. "Really?"

I nod. "I have a full scholarship. I wanted to study Latin, and the school in my neighborhood didn't offer it. Stony Hills has one hundred percent college acceptance into the top colleges around the country."

"So you are planning to go to college? Have you thought about it yet?"

"I always think about it," I admit. "I've been studying like crazy and making straight As so I can get a scholarship. There's three of us, so I don't think there's gonna be enough for all of us to attend college. My aunt Cerise promised me that she'd make sure I went, but she died over in Iraq. She was in the Army Reserves."

"I'm so sorry to hear about your aunt, dear. I know losing someone is never easy, but how proud you must be of her sacrifice for this country."

"I am proud of her, but I do miss her terribly."

"What are you planning on studying when you get to college?"

"Law," I answer. "I've always wanted to become a lawyer."

"My husband is an entertainment attorney. We met when I was in my first year of law school."

"So you're a lawyer, too?" I ask, trying to imagine her pacing back and forth in front of a stern-faced judge with that flaming, fire engine red hair.

"I dropped out when I got married. We wanted to have a family right away, and I wanted to be home with them. Plus, my love for the law was never as passionate as my husband's, so it was an easy decision for me."

"I'm about to make a food run," Lisa, a stylist, announces. "Give me your orders."

"Where are you going?" one of the other stylists asks. "I have a taste for Fatburgers."

"That sounds good," I say. "If that's where you're going, then I'll take a pastrami burger."

"I guess I'll be going to Fatburgers then," Lisa states as she sweeps up a cloud of hair from around her station. "Rhyann, would you write down everybody's order and call it in? I'd appreciate it."

I do as she asks, making sure that I have everything down correctly. "Here you are, Lisa."

"Thanks, Rhyann. You are on your job, girl. I really like having you around."

"I'm glad to hear that, Lisa. Matter of fact, why don't you take Rhyann with you?" Miss Marilee suggests. "She can help you with the orders."

I nod eagerly in agreement.

"Rhyann, you are such a pleasure to work with," Lisa says when we're in the car. "I'm so glad Marilee hired you."

"Thank you for saying that," I respond. "I really like working at the salon."

"All of the stylists have nothing but wonderful things to say about you. The clients, too."

"Even Mrs. Goldberg?"

Lisa chuckles. "She's a bit of a character, but for the most part, she's harmless."

"I see that now."

We drive for a few blocks before I ask, "Have you spoken to China? Her baby is so cute."

"She's so happy," Lisa assures me. "She and Mike really wanted this baby."

"I'm not sure I want kids."

Lisa glances over at me with a small smirk. "Well, that's really not something you should be worrying about, especially at your age."

"I'm definitely not giving it too much thought right now. I'm concentrating on finishing high school and planning for college."

"I can tell that you're very intelligent. Take it from me,

there's plenty of time for boys. They won't suddenly disappear off the face of the earth."

"My aunt tells me that all the time. She needs to remind my brother Brady that girls won't disappear overnight. He's really good in football, and he's being courted by several colleges across the country. If he's not careful, some hood rat is going to try and get caught up so that he'll have to pay child support, or worse—get married."

"That's what happened with my brother," Lisa tells me. "His little girlfriend got pregnant as soon as he was drafted into the NBA. They're married now, but I can tell he's not happy."

"Your brother plays for the Atlanta Hawks, right?"

She nods.

The food is ready and waiting by the time we arrive at Fatburgers. Lisa pays for the orders and we head back to the car.

"Everything smells delicious," I say. My stomach growls loudly in response, much to my embarrassment.

Lisa laughs. "I guess your belly agrees."

"That was so gross."

We make our way back to the salon, fighting traffic the whole way.

Lisa parks the car. "Seems like that took forever. I hope the food is still hot."

As I sit in the little break room in the back of the salon, eating my burger, I think back to my conversation with Mrs. Goldberg. Her mother was actually in a concentration camp.

I remember having to read *The Diary of Anne Frank* last year. It's hard to digest all that her mother suffered.

Mrs. Goldberg is right about us having so much in common. I'd never really thought about it before, and now I want to find out a whole lot more about it. Mrs. Goldberg will see. I can be a friend, too.

Chapter 12

$\mathcal{D}$id you know that blacks were victimized during the Holocaust?" I ask Divine when I call her later that evening. She has just told me about the grade she got on her report on slavery in the 1800s and the modern-day slavery in Rwanda.

"Those were the Jews, you silly." Divine breaks into a short laugh. "But I guess what our ancestors went through could be considered a holocaust, too."

"I know about the Jews," I correct her. "But it wasn't just the Jews who died. There were also some of us killed, Dee. This woman that comes to the salon—Mrs. Goldberg told me. She's a client of Miss Marilee."

Divine's voice fills with doubt. "Rhyann, I don't know about that. I've never heard anything about it."

"It's true," I say. "I was just looking up some information on the internet. Apparently, the French army had African soldiers during World War I. Some of them moved to Germany and fell in love with German women and had children. Well, Hitler had a problem with mixed-race children and warned that he'd have the blacks deported or placed in concentration camps."

"That man was totally evil," Divine cries. "I'm so glad he's dead. I hope God gets him good for all the pain and heartache he caused."

"He had the mixed-raced children and some of the grown-ups sterilized, saying he was preserving racial purity." I shake my head sadly. "It's bad enough that the black soldiers already had issues in the military, but if they were captured and taken to a concentration camp—Dee, they had it worse. They were treated less than the Jews."

"That's just dogged out."

I am outraged by what I read. "Mrs. Goldberg's mother was in one of the camps. She survived and came to America, where she met her husband and had a family."

"I was wondering why you were so interested in this."

"Girl, you know I have to stay up on my African American history," I respond. "Auntie Mo always tells me that if we don't search for our history, we won't find a thing about it. My history teacher never once mentioned there being any blacks in the Holocaust. She mentioned the old people, the homosexuals and how they were treated, but she never said anything about black people. I can't wait to go to school tomorrow, because I'm bringing it up."

"Rhyann, you're not gonna confront your teacher about black history, are you?"

"Not confront her like that, but I *am* going to ask her why it was never mentioned that blacks were sent to concentration camps. Girl, that's deep. We need to know about our people. We didn't just show up right before slavery and then disappear when it was all over."

"I know that's right," Dee says. "I'm going online tonight to find out what I can about this."

"That's what I did. I'm ordering this book titled *Valaida* from Amazon. The author is Candace Allen. Valaida was a jazz musician and singer. She was arrested and sent to a concentration camp."

"I'll order one, too. Maybe we can read it together and discuss. I'll see if Alyssa wants a copy. You should tell Mimi about it," Divine suggests.

"Not," I say. "You know she won't be interested in nothing like this. If it's not shopping or boys, she's not interested."

We laugh.

"So, how are things going between you and T. J.?" I ask.

"Good," Divine responds. "We're taking it one day at a time."

"Aren't you scared to give your heart to someone else after all that Madison put you through?" I ask.

"Yeah, in a way, but life is all about chances, Rhyann."

I can't agree with that. "I don't like hurting."

"That's like saying you don't like breathing," Divine points out. "Rhyann, it's going to happen, and there's nothing you can do about it. Believe me, I know."

"Life can be so hard at times," I say barely above a whisper.

"But it can be fun, too," Divine interjects. "Like when I get to Los Angeles. We are going to have so much fun . . . hey, hold on for a minute. I hear my aunt Phoebe calling me for something."

I hum to the music playing on the radio in my room while waiting for Divine to come back on the line.

When she does, she is upset. "Jerome called earlier. Ava's having some more problems. She has to stay in bed until she has the baby now."

"Do they know what's wrong?"

"My aunt says that she keeps going into labor and it's too soon. If Ava has the baby now, she might not live."

"Who?" I want to know. "Ava or the baby?"

"The baby," Divine responds crossly.

"Are you okay?"

She catches herself, softens her tone. "Yeah. I'm going to pray for them when we get off the phone."

"I'll pray for them too," I tell her. "Don't worry, Dee. The baby is gonna be fine. You'll see."

"I hope so," she murmurs.

I know that Divine isn't crazy about Ava, but she is truly worried about her baby sister. She already loves that little girl.

"Kyle was so mean to me last night," Mimi announces while we're waiting for the first bell to ring.

"What did you do to make him mad at you?" I ask.

She shrugs. "That's just it, Rhyann. I don't know. All I did was call him to see if he was going to pick me up this morning for school. I was going to start riding with him."

"Did he ask you to ride with him?"

"No, but I don't see why we can't," Mimi responds. "He's my boyfriend."

I see the problem, and I push a little harder. "Did you ask him if you could ride to school with him?"

Mimi shakes her head no. "Why should I have to ask?"

"That's probably why he's mad with you," I say.

She nods quickly, seeing it, too. She takes a sip of the Starbucks chai tea that she loves so much. "Rhyann, I've done everything I can think of to make that boy happy. I don't know why I keep messing up." Lowering her voice to a whisper, she adds, "The only time he seems happy with me is when we're being romantic. He loves to kiss."

I back away. "You could've kept that to yourself."

"Don't hate, Rhyann," Mimi murmurs with a giggle. "I can't help it if he loves my lips."

I survey her face, and then my eyes travel down to her neck. "Looks like Kyle is a vampire."

Her hand flies upward, trying to hide the purplish area with her collar. "Can you still see it?"

"Not as much," I answer. "Did your mom see it?"

"No, thank goodness. She would've had a fit. I told Kyle he can't be leaving hickeys on my neck like that."

"I guess you two are getting hot and heavy."

Mimi breaks into a grin. "We are."

"Well, just remember our pledge. We're members of the 'V' Club until we say our wedding vows."

She is dismayed that I reminded her. "Rhyann, that's really hard. I don't know why we made that stupid pledge anyway. Kyle says that nobody is waiting until marriage to have sex."

"I am," I respond. "So are Divine and Alyssa. Kyle doesn't know what he's talking about."

"Okay, so that's three people."

"What about you, Mimi? Are you still a card-carrying member?"

The bell rings.

"I see Kyle. I need to talk to him," Mimi says before rushing off.

I note that she never answered my question, but I'm not about to let it go. She and Kyle make a nice couple, but no way are they ready for sex.

No way.

But I can't help but wonder if it's already too late to have that talk with my girl.

Chapter 13

$\mathcal{A}$fter school, I shift my backpack from one side to the other while I wait on Mimi. We need to finish our discussion from earlier. I'm not about to let her sweep this discussion under the rug.

"I had to stop by my locker after class," she tells me.

I get right to the point. "You never did answer my question, Mimi. Are you and Kyle having sex?"

She blushes guiltily for a moment before responding, "No, we're not."

I'm not quite sure I believe her. She doesn't seem to be able to look me directly in the eye. "You don't have to lie to me, Mimi."

"I'm not lying. I don't have to lie to you."

"Don't get an attitude," I say. "You made the vow just like I did. We're supposed to ask these kinds of questions. It's how we keep each other on track."

Mimi sits down on a nearby bench. "I know."

I hold up my hands. "If you want me out of your business, then just say so."

She shakes her head. "It's fine, Rhyann. I haven't had sex with Kyle, but I'll admit, he does want to. Kyle says he wants to get really close to me and that's the only way."

"He's not your husband, so he doesn't need to be any closer," I tell her. "He might not be the man you end up marrying."

"But then again, we might be together forever," Mimi pleads. "It's possible."

"Yeah," I say. "But I wouldn't bet on it."

Divine, Alyssa, Mimi, and I made a pact that we would hold each other accountable when it comes to the "V" Club. I don't want Mimi getting so wrapped up in high school love that she gets caught up in something she's not mature enough to handle.

I sound like Auntie Mo right now, but she's right about this. I know I'm not ready for that.

My stomach is in knots.

Today after church, I have to audition for a spot on the Temple of Praise squad. I've been practicing my routine for the past two weeks, and I'm pretty sure I have a good chance of making it.

I see Kelly shortly after we arrive. I can't believe this. She's actually pretending that she doesn't have a clue who I am.

I shake it off with a chuckle. I'm not gonna let her get to me.

Auntie Mo pulls me off to the side and asks, "What's going on between you and Kelly?"

"She's mad because I'm auditioning for the praise team."

"That's a shame," she whispers. "Well, shrug it off and pray for her."

"I will."

We enter the sanctuary and take our seats for the morning service.

Two hours later, I walk over to the administration building with Tameka for the audition. My sister has come for moral support. Auntie Mo has a meeting with the other women on the committee with her. They are coordinating the pastoral appreciation luncheon.

I'm not surprised to find Kelly already there. She rolls her eyes before turning away from me in her seat.

"Did you see that?" Tameka asks.

I flip my hand in nonchalance. "Let her trip."

We sit down and wait for the auditions to begin. Four of us are trying out.

The first person is called to do her routine. She is so clumsy that Tameka puts her head down to keep from laughing out loud.

I send her a sharp glare. She's so wrong.

The next person is up. I'm not trying to talk about anybody, but didn't she at least try to learn the routine?

It's Kelly's turn. She does a pretty decent job, but I feel confident that I can still show her up.

I'm next. I say a quick prayer and then perform to CeCe Winans's "Waging War."

When I'm done, I walk back to my seat. Tameka leans over to whisper in my ear, "Sis, you were fierce. I know you got this."

We won't find out for a couple of days, because the leaders want to pray over their decision. At least that's what they tell us. I don't miss the way one of them keeps looking at Kelly and smiling when she thinks no one is looking.

I don't want to be negative, but I have a feeling that Kelly will be the new Temple of Praise dancer. Sometimes life just isn't fair.

Mimi calls me shortly after I return home. "How did the audition go?" she asks.

"I was pretty good," I say. "But I think they're going to give it to another girl."

"The one you told me about?"

"Yeah." I sit down on the edge of my bed. "I'll be okay with it if she's not the one who gets the spot. I'm tired of her winning everything."

"Maybe you're wrong. You might get it, Rhyann."

"I hope so," I murmur.

"Rhyann, I need you to do me a big favor."

I pick up my remote control and turn the TV on. "What?"

"Kyle wants to introduce you to one of his boys. He wants us to double-date."

I shake my head vigorously. "Not interested."

"Please, Rhyann," Mimi pleads. "It's just dinner on a Thursday night. We won't be out late or anything. Just meet his friend. If you don't like him, then you'll never have to see him again."

I keep shaking my head even though she can't see me. "Mimi, I'm not into blind dates."

"Just do this for me. Kyle is really excited about this. I love when he's like this, Rhyann. He's not acting so moody. He even went out and bought me a new Gucci watch."

"He did what?" I ask, an octave higher than normal.

"He gave me a Gucci watch. I've been waiting for you to notice it. I'll show it to you tomorrow."

I'm in shock. What is this chick thinking?

"I can't believe you took such an expensive gift from Kyle. Mimi, that's a lot of money."

"He likes spending money on me."

I can't help but ask, "Are your parents okay with this?"

"I haven't told them," she admits. "Rhyann, he's my boyfriend. I don't see where it's such a big deal."

"And what do you think he's gonna want in return, Mimi?"

"Duuh . . . he wants me."

"In bed," I say.

Her voice goes all light and airy. "Rhyann, I know you're bitter, but don't try to push all that on me. I'm not afraid to have a relationship. If it doesn't work out, I'll just find another boyfriend. I got it like that."

"Whatever . . ."

"Anyway, don't think you're changing the subject on me. I really need you to be the B.F.F. you're supposed to be and go on that double date with me. Besides, if you're so worried that Kyle is out for my goodies, you can be there to block."

I sigh in resignation. "You just had to pull the B.F.F. card. Fine, Mimi, I'll go on this date with you, but it won't be on Thursday. I need to finish my history research paper and my final science project."

"Rhyann, I love you, girl."

"No, you owe me big time," I counter. "I plan on collecting, too."

I put Mimi off for two weeks.

After turning in my assignments, she brings up the promise I made. I reluctantly agree to go out with them on Saturday night.

I can't believe I let Mimi talk me into going on a blind date with a friend of Kyle's. Also, my aunt has no idea that Mimi and I are meeting boys at a restaurant. She likes to meet the boy and his parents before I go anywhere with him.

Since it's a blind date, I didn't want to go through all that drama, so I just said Mimi and I were going out to dinner. It's what I would call a half-truth.

Auntie Mo would call it a straight-up lie.

I send up a silent prayer that she won't ever find out about this. The last thing I want is to be grounded so close to summer break. Auntie Mo will find a way to make my life miserable.

Mimi picks me up at seven thirty.

"Don't stay out too late, Rhyann," Auntie Mo says.

"I won't," I promise her.

Once we're in Mimi's BMW, she tells me, "You're really going to like Gage. His father owns Tenez Records. I didn't know he was friends with Kyle until Kyle told me right before I left the house." She flashes me a big grin. "Rhyann, he's so cute."

"So why would I like him exactly?" I ask while playing with my necklace. "I already can't stand his name. Who names their child Gage? Nobody I know."

"Rhyann, don't start," Mimi says. "I need you to be nice tonight. Gage really wants to meet you because he's heard all this wonderful stuff from Kyle."

"Is he black?" I ask. "Maybe you don't mind jumping across the color lines, but I love my black brothers."

"Yes, Gage is African American. Does that make you feel better, Rhyann?" A hurt tone creeps into her voice. "I thought you liked Kyle."

"I do like him," I respond. "I think he's really nice. *For you*. All that blond hair would just work my nerves. Although he's got the prettiest blue eyes I've seen."

Mimi flashes that big smile of hers. "I really like him."

I chuckle. "Mimi, I *know* that." I shift in the seat, watching the cars out the window. "Look, I don't care who you date as long as he treats you right. He could be green or purple for all I care. Then again, that would be a little strange if you start dating a green or purple person. I love me some purple but not in my men."

She laughs. "You're stupid."

She parks the car across the street from the restaurant. "Rhyann, leave all of your negative vibes out here, okay? Let's have a good time."

"What are you trying to say, Mimi?" I demand. "I'm not a negative person—just a realist."

She flings her Gucci purse across her shoulder and heads toward the restaurant. "Call it whatever you want, just don't bring it into the restaurant. I totally want to enjoy our evening with Kyle and Gage."

Whatever. I'm not gonna be a fake person. If he gets on my nerves, I'll call my cousin to pick me up in a flash.

We're escorted to our table as soon as we walk inside.

Gage isn't bad-looking at all. I even find myself warming up to him until I realize just how much he adores talking about himself.

The waitress comes to take our drink orders.

I could hug her, I'm so glad to have this break from hearing more about Gage. The truth is that I stopped listening to him a while back. Even though Traven is a playa, I think I'd rather be with him right now.

After the waitress comes back with our drinks, I give her my food selection, then push away from the table saying, "Excuse me. I need to go to the girls' room." I rise to my feet.

Mimi gets up, too. "I'll go with you."

As soon as we step inside the bathroom, she confronts me. "Can you, like, stop looking so doggone bored, Rhyann?"

I give Mimi a hard look. "Maybe if I wasn't bored—"

"You're ruining things for me and Kyle. Just try and be nice to Gage, please."

"I *am* being nice, Mimi. I'm sorry, but all he wants to do is talk about himself. I know who his father is. I know that he thinks being the prince of the Tenez Records empire is a big deal, but I'm not impressed."

"Please, Rhyann . . . ," Mimi pleads. "Be nice."

I'm quickly losing my temper. "I didn't want to come on this date in the first place. I'm not going to be rude, but you better find a way to shut him up. I don't want to hear another word from Gage about who he is or what he has."

"What am I supposed to do?" Mimi asks. "It's not like I can tell him to shut up and quit talking about himself."

"If you don't, then I will."

Mimi looks like she's about to cry. She starts pacing back and forth in the ladies' room. "I knew it. I even told Kyle that this wasn't going to work. Rhyann, I really did, but he wanted to do it anyway. *Can we please just get through the dinner?*"

Only because Mimi's my girl and I'd never do anything to embarrass her, I say, "Okay, I'll be nice. But you tell Kyle that I don't need any help in the dating department, okay? Besides, he met Traven."

"But he knows that you're not dating him."

I fold my arms across my chest. "How does he know that?"

Mimi takes a step back. "I kind of told him. I'm sorry, Rhyann. I didn't think it was a secret or anything."

I take my time checking out my reflection in the mirror. "Let's just get through this evening, but Mimi, don't be discussing my personal life with your boyfriend. I hope we're clear on this."

"I really thought you and Gage would hit it off."

"Then that should've been your first clue that this wasn't gonna work out."

We return to our table.

"You okay?" I hear Kyle ask Mimi.

She nods.

I can tell she's not very happy with me right now, but I'm not pressed about it. Mimi knows how I am and she knows that I definitely don't care for blind dates. I'll get through the evening, and then I never have to see Gage again.

I'm totally surprised to see China when I enter the salon on Friday.

"You're back at work already?" I ask her. It's only been what, a couple of weeks since she had little Gabriella? I thought women had to be out at least six weeks before they could do anything.

"Oh, no . . . I just came to drop something off for Mom. I needed to run some errands, so since Mike is on paternity leave, I left him home with the baby."

The door blows open and all I see is a flash of red.

Mrs. Goldberg is actually ten minutes early for her hair appointment. I'm shocked, because she usually runs late.

"Rhyann, I'm glad you're here," she says. She hands me a can of my favorite toffee-ettes. "I brought you some candy."

"Mrs. G, you're trying to make me fat, aren't you?" I ask, accepting her gift. "You just hating on me because I'm giving you some competition. I like those jeans you have on, but you know they'd look fierce on me."

She laughs. "I think they look pretty fierce on me."

"Mrs. G, why are you always bringing candy for Rhyann?" China asks. "You making the rest of us in here feel like you don't like us no more."

She smiles and holds up a gift-wrapped box. "I didn't forget my ladies here. I brought lots of candy. There's enough for everybody. China, what on earth are you doing here? You are still recovering from childbirth."

"I had to run some errands. I'm going back home as soon as Mom gets back. By the way, thanks so much for the beautiful blanket, Mrs. G. It's so soft and just gorgeous."

"You're welcome, dear. I hope you brought me a picture of that beautiful baby girl."

China reaches for her purse. "I sure did. I came by here

to leave it with my mom. But since you're here, I can give it directly to you. Miss G, where did you get those shoes? I love them."

"Aren't they cute?" Mrs. Goldberg responds. "I bought them last year at Saks."

"Those are some nice shoes for real."

Without waiting for Miss Marilee, I escort Mrs. Goldberg back to the shampoo bowl and get her ready to get her hair washed.

"Miss Marilee will be back any minute. She had to run to the bank."

"Not a problem. She probably thought I'd be late as usual. I probably would, but lately I've been confused when I drive, so my husband dropped me off today."

That doesn't sound good. "Are you still having those headaches?"

"They are becoming more frequent lately."

"Mrs. G, when are you going to let a doctor check you out?"

"When I can no longer stand the pain," she responds with a smile. "How are things with you, dear?"

"Okay," I reply with a slight edge. "Things are going better today than they did last weekend."

"What happened last weekend, if you don't mind me asking?"

"I went on a blind date with my B.F.F. and her boyfriend Saturday," I tell Mrs. Goldberg.

"It doesn't sound like you had a good time."

"I didn't," I confirm. "My so-called date got on my last

nerve. He was so arrogant and kept bragging about his father's record company and all of his celebrity friends."

She tilts her head up slightly to catch my eye. "Think you'll be seeing this young man again?"

I shake my head. "No, ma'am. He was nice and all, Miss G, but I'm not interested in him in that way." I release a long sigh. "I don't think I'll ever have another boyfriend. Too much drama."

"Dear, just focus on your education for now. The world will not run out of boys, I assure you. Baby boys are born every day."

I laugh before asking, "Do you have children?"

"No, dear. I was never so fortunate. I really wanted them, but it just wasn't in the plan for me."

"Mrs. G, I think you would've been a great mother."

She smiles. "I always thought so, too."

Miss Marilee arrives just as I rinse the shampoo out of Mrs. Goldberg's hair.

They chat for a few minutes while I apply the leave-in conditioner.

Miss Marilee escorts Mrs. Goldberg to her chair while I grab a slice of lemon cake and her favorite latte. She doesn't tip, and I don't look for one.

I have five more clients to shampoo before I leave for the day.

Auntie Mo picks me up, and we drive over to the church. She needs to take some measurements for the costumes she's going to make for an upcoming play the teens at church are performing. I offer to help her by writing everything down.

My stomach sinks when I find that Kelly's been given the spot with Temple of Praise. I had a feeling it was gonna go down this way, so I shouldn't be surprised.

"I'm so sorry," Auntie Mo tells me.

"It's okay," I say. "I'm not going to let this get me down."

Deep down, though, I feel like crying, because I really wanted to be a member of the praise team.

We head home after we leave the church.

"Brady got into USC," Auntie Mo announces during the drive. "Praise the Lord, he was given a full ride. He got an athletic scholarship."

That brightens up my day in a flash. "That's wonderful," I say.

Auntie Mo nods happily. "Thank you, God . . . Thank you . . ."

Auntie Mo stops at the grocery store to buy a cake for dessert. Tonight is going to be a celebration. I guess Brady will be getting his car for sure now.

As for me . . . I won't be dancing before the Lord. All the stuff that Kelly did to me comes back into my mind.

It's not fair that she can get away with her schemes while I'm trying to live right. Life sucks big-time.

Auntie Mo comes to my bedroom shortly after I finish my homework.

"I know you're disappointed," she tells me.

"Kelly has stolen my ideas before and now she's on Temple of Praise. To be honest, she's not a real nice person—she uses people. Auntie Mo, it's not fair."

"Maybe God has something else for you, Rhyann." She places a warm hand on my shoulder. "Everything happens for a reason, whether we think it's fair or not. You just keep doing the right thing and stop worrying about Kelly. For every action, there is a consequence."

I hear what Auntie Mo is saying, but the verses are not working for me right now. All I can see is that Kelly's won again.

Why did I have to lose to her, of all people?

Chapter 14

I've been thinking about how you're going to pay me back for going on that date with *Mr. My father owns a record company and that makes me special,*" I tell Mimi on Saturday. "I've finally figured out a way. I want you to come with me to the Museum of Tolerance. The way I see it, you owe me big time."

She frowns at the idea. "Why in the world do you want to go there? I'm in the mood for something fun."

Mimi can be so dense sometimes. "I want to learn more about the Holocaust," I explain. "That boy got on my last nerve, Mimi, so pay up."

"I didn't think Gage was that bad."

"That's because you didn't really have to deal with him. You were all up in Kyle's face."

Mimi bows her head in resignation. "Fine. I'll pay up. When do you want to go?"

"How about later today?"

"Rhyann, I wanted to go to the mall," Mimi whines. "Why don't we do it next Saturday?"

"You owe me, remember?" I remind her. "Besides, Brady's graduation party is that day."

"Fine . . . we can go today. But we're meeting Kyle and Gage later this evening. Okay?"

"Not okay," I say. "Mimi, I'm not interested in the golden boy of Tenez Records. Sorry, but I really don't want to spend another minute around him."

"Please, Rhyann . . ."

"Mimi, you're going to the museum with me as payback for the last date from you-know-where. If I go on another one, you're gonna have to give me your car."

She gives me a long-suffering look. "Can't I just treat you to a spa day, Rhyann?"

"Kyle must be some kisser," I say, watching her closely. I'm beginning to think that Mimi and Kyle have been getting closer than close. "It's gone beyond kissing."

Mimi doesn't respond.

"What are you thinking?"

Her answer comes out all in a rush. "We haven't gone all the way, Rhyann. Kyle says that what we're doing is okay."

"So now you're taking your boyfriend's advice about how far to go?" I try to keep my disappointment in Mimi out of my voice.

"We're just touching each other. There's nothing wrong with that," she says, getting defensive. "Besides, it's so hard to say no to him sometimes."

"If you keep it up, it's gonna lead to more, Mimi. He's not gonna want to leave it at that, and you probably won't either."

"Rhyann, you can yell at me later. Right now let's talk about you and Gage. He really wants to spend time with you and he keeps bugging Kyle about it. It's his best friend, so what is he supposed to do?"

My volume dials up a notch. "Learn how to say no, for one thing. Mimi, I can't stand Gage. I'm sorry, but I don't want to go out with him again."

"He's rich," she tells me.

"And?"

"Rhyann, please do this for me?"

"I can't." I don't care how much she begs, I'm not going out with Gage. I already know she's not going to give up this easily, but Kyle and I differ in that respect. "Mimi, I know how to say no and mean it."

"Rhyann, that wasn't nice."

"It's the truth," I retort. "Anyway, you're not getting out of going to the museum with me. You owe me. And since you're having such a hard time saying no, you won't refuse me."

Mimi can be such a pain sometimes.

She whines all the way to the museum that she's going to be so bored. "I hate stuff like this, Rhyann, but I'm sacrificing myself for you. Why can't you do the same for me?"

"I already did—that's how you ended up here with me. If you'd like to hand over your car keys, then we might be able to negotiate something."

"I can't believe you're being so mean."

"Believe it. It's true."

We get out of her car and head inside.

Mimi and I get in line with the other visitors for the tour shortly after we arrive.

"I can't believe I let you talk me into coming here," Mimi complains. "I should've just bought you some See's candy and called it a day."

"That wouldn't have worked this time," I say.

At the start of the tour, we each receive a photo passport card with the story of a child whose life was transformed by the events of the Holocaust. We won't find out what happened to the child until the end of the tour. Mimi's attention shifts, captured by the photo passport in her hand. "I wonder what happened to this little boy," she murmurs.

I stare at the photo of the little dark-haired girl with the big eyes on my own passport. Although this happened so long ago and I don't know this little girl, I find myself praying that she survived.

We move from one exhibit to the next, reliving decades of

events in Germany, from before World War II, through the rise and fall of the Third Reich, to the liberation.

Mimi and I break down in tears as we listen to the unforgettable stories of Holocaust survivors in the Hall of Testimony.

At the end of the exhibit, we find out what happened to the children on the cards.

"He died, Rhyann," Mimi whispers. Tears stream down her face. "That poor little boy died. They exterminated him as if he was a bug. It's so wrong."

Her face is all red and her eyes are wet. Mimi's truly upset about this, and I'm surprised. Usually she's caught up in her own world. I wrap an arm around her, horrified to find that that beautiful little boy was gassed in Auschwitz. "I just hope that he wasn't alone."

"Me, too," Mimi whimpers. "How can people be so mean? A lot of the prisoners were just little children. Who would they hurt?"

I wanted to know the answer to that question myself.

"Aren't you going to find out what happened to your child?" Mimi asks, reaching into her purse and pulling out a tissue. She wipes her face.

"I'm scared," I say. "I don't want to lose her. I know how crazy this sounds, but I want to remember her like this."

Mimi takes my hand. "We have to find out. We'll always wonder if we don't."

I insert my passport.

"She survived," I say with a huge sigh of relief. "She made it. I don't think I could've handled another death right now."

∽

Tuesday afternoon, Mrs. Goldberg brings her mother to the salon. She introduces her, saying, "This is my mother, Rivka Braddock."

"It's so nice to meet you, Mrs. Braddock," I respond with a smile. "I've heard a lot about you."

She shakes my hand, her grip firm. "Ann has told me quite a bit about you, too. It's a pleasure to meet you, Rhyann."

"I told Mother how interested you were in the Holocaust and that you've been doing some research."

"My friend and I went to the Museum of Tolerance on Saturday," I announce. "I'm so glad I went."

"Mother and I are members."

"I attended an event there just last week," Mrs. Braddock tells me. "They had Eva Brown there. She is a survivor and the author of *If You Save One Life*."

"I would've liked to attend something like that," I say. "It sounds pretty interesting."

"It was," Mrs. Braddock says. "I think you would've enjoyed it."

My eyes travel down to her arm, where I can glimpse the numbers marring her skin. She catches me staring and says, "Shortly after I stepped off the train in Auschwitz, they tattooed this number on my arm." She pushes up her sleeve to give me a better view. "They gave me number four-six-two-four-two." She goes on to explain, "The separate numbers add up to eighteen. In the Hebrew language, the letters of the alphabet also stand for numbers. The letters making up the number eighteen spell out the Hebrew word *chai,* which means 'life.' I always believed that this was God's way of showing me that despite what happened, from that moment forward I would survive."

"Did you see the crematorium?"

She nods. "The crematorium was just a few minutes away from the barracks where I slept. We could see the chimneys, and we could smell the gas from the gas chambers. It was a terrible smell—the burning of the bodies." Her eyes tear up at the memory.

"You don't have to talk about it if it upsets you," I say, although I desperately want to hear the rest of her story.

"No, we must never forget. I'm fine," Mrs. Braddock responds. She straightens up to her full height. "When it was over, they cleared the grates. From where we were sleeping, we could hear the grates being cleaned. It's very similar to what your own oven would be like when you move the grates around, except that it was much noisier. To this very day when I clean my own oven, I'm reminded of that noise of the cleaning of the grates in the crematorium."

"I read about how they crammed people in there," I say, feeling sick to my stomach. "Then on top of that, they stuffed little kids on top of them. Is all that true?"

She nods. "I'm afraid so. I saw when the transports came. I saw them throw living children into the crematorium. They would grab them by an arm and a leg and throw them in. The guards were cruel men."

"My friend's passport had the picture of a little boy, and we found out that he was gassed. They were so cruel to kids, and I don't understand why."

God, why would you let this happen? Why did these people have to suffer and die like this?

Miss Marilee gets my attention to let me know that I have to shampoo her client. I hate having to put my conversation with Mrs. Braddock on hold, but I am here to do a job.

While I wash the client's hair, Miss Marilee gets started on Mrs. Braddock. I can hear Mrs. G giving instructions on how she wants her mother's hair trimmed and styled.

When I'm done, I sit in China's chair and listen as Mrs. Braddock continues her story.

"When they arrived, the American soldiers were very nice. Right off they cooked rice for us. I was so hungry, but when one of the soldiers saw me take some rice, he said, 'You can't eat that. If you do, you might die. There is too much fat in that for you.' He explained that my stomach had shrunk. He gave me a piece of bread and suggested that I toast it before eating it. I had no idea what he meant." Mrs. Braddock chuckles. "The nice man had to tell me that toast is when you make bread hard."

I smile.

"Are you in contact with other survivors?" Miss Marilee asks.

Mrs. Braddock nods. "We attended the World Gathering of Holocaust Survivors back in 1985. Several of us from Los Angeles went there together. We met survivors, relatives of survivors—"

"I went with her and my father," Mrs. Goldberg interjects. "It was an incredibly moving experience."

"Yes, it was," Mrs. Braddock tells me. "Many of the survivors got up and shared their experiences. Some were worse than others, but we were all survivors. Some would ask if there was anyone there from this town or that place. It was heartbreaking to see people still searching for family and friends after all this time."

"That's what slavery did to our people," I hear Miss Marilee say. "It broke up families. They really believed in the idea of 'united we stand and divided we fall.' That's what they were afraid of—that's why they separated us. I get it now."

"I used to wonder why I survived. I even felt guilty about surviving when my mother and my sister didn't."

"I tell Mother all the time that she's here because she's supposed to be alive," Mrs. Goldberg puts in. "Why is she still here? It's because she fought for her life. Some people believe that what will be, will be, but I don't agree. You have to fight for yourself day by day. My mother wanted to live and she held onto that will until the camp was liberated. That's how she survived. A person has to hold on to his own will, hold on to that until the very last minute."

I wipe away a tear. "Mrs. Braddock, I'm so glad you made it through that horrible time, and I'm so sorry you suffered like that. I never went through slavery, so I can't even say I can relate to anything you've said."

She reaches out and takes my hand. "My dear, it is my prayer that you never know the pain and suffering I've known just because of your skin color or who you are."

I give her a hug and then I walk over to Mrs. Goldberg to embrace her as well. "Thank you so much for bringing in your mother. I'm so glad I met her."

"You can never move forward without knowing the past."

"I'll see you next week." As I pull away, a thought pops up in my head. "Oh, my brother is going to USC. He got a full athletic scholarship."

Mrs. Goldberg claps her hands, and her brown eyes light up. "That's wonderful!"

Later at home, I tell Auntie Mo about Rivka Braddock.

"Auntie Mo, they killed her entire family. I wouldn't blame her if she hated all Germans."

My aunt draws back at my news, then takes a seat next to me. "Rhyann, hate is a choice. It's something that you choose to do. This woman chose to forgive instead. It takes a bigger person to do that."

"But look what happened to her," I argue. "Doesn't she have a right to hate? What about how what our ancestors suffered?"

"I'm not minimizing what our ancestors went through, nor how the Jews suffered, but think about Jesus Christ and his persecution. Are we no better than Him? He died for us, Rhyann. How can we not forgive when Christ died for our sins?"

My protests quiet down with her wise response. She always knows what to say. "I guess when you put it that way—it makes sense, but to be honest, I was hoping to hold on to my anger just a little while longer."

She smiles. "Okay, I'll give you five minutes, and then you have to let it go. But mind you, we don't know when the Lord's gonna peel back the sky. It could be at any time, and you don't want to be caught with unforgiveness in your heart."

I glance upward, just in case. "I'm not angry and I forgive all those murderers who tried to destroy the Jews." I get louder as I add, "I forgive those ignorant slave owners who used my people, bred them like animals, and then broke up the families."

"Are you sure you're in a forgiving mode?" Auntie Mo asks with a chuckle.

"I forgive everybody who isn't smart enough to know that skin color doesn't make a person less human. We have so much in common—if we'd only try to get along."

Auntie Mo wraps an arm around me. "You're absolutely right, sweetie."

We sit like that for a moment. Then a very good idea comes to me.

"Auntie Mo, I've been thinking . . . I think it's time we start looking for a car for me. When we go back to school, I don't want you having to drive me to school on your days off. You should enjoy your free time."

"Really?"

I nod. "I'm not looking for anything new."

"That's good, because I'm not either," Auntie Mo replies.

"Rhyann, you don't have to worry about me. I don't mind driving you to school. It's not a problem."

"In other words, you're not buying me a car anytime soon, right?"

"Right," she confirms.

"I'm gonna have to try and forgive you for that, Auntie Mo. That's a pretty big one, I want you to know."

She laughs, full-out this time.

Chapter 15

I have been waiting for this day since school started back in September. It's the last day of school.

Laughing and talking, Mimi and I breeze through the lunch line. After getting our food, we head to the picnic tables outside, deciding to enjoy the sunshine.

"I can actually sleep in tomorrow," Mimi says with a grin. "I'm so tired of school and having to get up early, Rhyann."

I totally understand, because I'm feeling the same way. "I know what you mean. No getting up early and no homework for the next couple of months. YES!!"

"Can you believe it? Dee and Alyssa will be here in a

couple of days. We're going to have such a good time being together again." Mimi takes a sip of her soda. "I can't wait."

"The first thing I want to do is spend a day at the beach—just the four of us. Remember how much fun we had last summer when they were here?"

She nods eagerly. "We did have fun. It was funny watching you trying not to get your hair wet. Who goes to the beach after getting a perm?"

"Well, I wanted to go," I say, not so pleased with the memory. "I didn't plan on getting into the water. That was all you and Dee."

Mimi laughs. "I don't think I'd ever seen you so mad when Dee splashed that water on you."

"Oh, I was hot!" I cry, but I'm smiling, too. "She paid to get my hair done the next day, but I was still a little upset with her. That was just plain wrong."

"You know that she didn't mean to get your hair wet," Mimi says.

"It doesn't matter now," I respond. "I know how you and Dee are, so this time I'm gonna be prepared. I'm getting braids for the summer."

"When are you getting them done?" she asks.

"Next Friday," I respond. "Marcella is going to do them for me."

"Is she back?" Mimi wants to know. "I haven't seen her at the salon the last two or three times I was getting my hair done."

"She came back two days ago." Marcella had a baby two

months ago and recently returned from her maternity leave. She is the only one in the salon who braids hair, so she was missed. I'm glad she agreed to do mine. Hopefully, I can keep it like that all summer and take them out right before we go back to school.

"You know, Gage keeps asking Kyle about you," Mimi tells me. "I think he's into you, girl."

"I hope not," I say with a frown. "I don't like him."

"You haven't even gotten to know him, Rhyann. You keep saying that you're not into Traven, so what's really going on with you?"

I'm not getting dragged into all this. "Mimi, I know enough about Kyle's friend to know that he's not really my type. As for me and Traven . . . well, there's nothing to tell." I really hope she doesn't start tripping on me because I'm not interested in her boo's friend. He's so not my type.

"Just go out with him one more time, please . . ."

I meet her gaze straight on. "Why? Why is it so important to you, Mimi? Does Kyle have that much control over you?"

A spark of anger flashes in her eyes, but it quickly disappears. "You might change your mind if you give yourself a chance to get to know him."

I shake my head. "I'll pass."

A tense moment passes before she decides to change the subject. "What time is the graduation?"

"It's at seven. We're leaving at six fifteen so that we can get some seats as close to the front as possible."

Mimi hands me a card. "This is for Brady."

"Why don't you wait and just give this to him tomorrow at the party?" I ask.

"Oh, yeah. I can do that."

I finish up my lunch. "Mimi, I need to go to the Baldwin Hills Crenshaw Plaza after school. I have to get a shirt for the pants I'm wearing tonight. The shirt I bought is too big. I'm not going to be able to ride to Beverly Hills with you."

"I'll go with you," she tells me. "I want to find something for the party tomorrow."

"All you need are a pair of jeans and a shirt. It's not a black-tie event, so don't think too hard on it."

"I still want to look nice. Kyle's coming with me. That's okay, right?"

I shrug. "I don't care, and I don't think Auntie Mo will mind. She even invited your parents, but I know they're not coming."

"Only because my father has to be in Chicago. He's getting an award from the college he attended there."

"I'm surprised you and your mom aren't going with him. It sounds like a big deal."

"My mom was going to go, but he told her that she didn't have to. He knows how much my mother hates traveling these days." She sounds puzzled. "I don't know what happened, but she just wants to stay home. I think she's depressed about something."

You think? I still don't get why Mimi can't see what is happening in her own house. Maybe Divine and I should have a talk with her this summer.

The bell rings.

"Two more classes," I groan. "I wish this day was over already."

"Me, too," Mimi contributes.

We slowly make our way to fifth period.

Brady and Traven are graduating tonight. I hope they realize just how lucky they are. I'm so ready to get out of high school, although I don't have a clue what I'd do after that. I'm still trying to decide where I want to go to school and what I want to major in. I am strongly considering Spelman University in Atlanta. I do know that whatever I decide, it'll be an HBCU (Historically Black College or University).

We practically run out of school at the end of the day.

School's out for the summer!

Mimi and I head straight for the mall.

"Is there an Old Navy in here?" Mimi asks.

"No."

"Then why are we here?"

"Because we're going to New York & Company."

Mimi wears a look of confusion. "What do they have there? I don't think I've ever been in one of those."

"You'll see. I keep forgetting how sheltered you've been," I say with a laugh.

"Ha-ha . . . you're so funny," she retorts.

"This is New York & Company," I announce. "I get some of my clothes from here. The outfit I'm wearing to Brady's graduation came from here."

Mimi glances around the store. "They have some cute things in here."

"I know. That's why I shop in this store. See, you can still be fashionable and not spend hundreds of dollars."

I stroll over to a nearby rack, looking for the shirt I want but in the right size this time.

"Are you going to just stare at the shirt, or do you plan on buying it anytime soon?" Mimi asks.

I don't look up. "What's your hurry?"

"I told Kyle I'd call him when I was on my way."

"I haven't decided yet," I tell her. "You can leave if you want, Mimi."

"I don't want to leave here like that."

"It's not a problem," I tell her. "Really, I can catch the bus home from here. I'll see you later."

She's not happy about it, but she heads to the store entrance. Then she stops and turns around. "Hey, I thought you were gonna ride with me to Beverly Hills."

"Mimi, go on and meet Kyle. I need to find something to wear for my brother's graduation, which is in a few hours. I'll see you tomorrow."

"You sure you're okay with me leaving?" she asks.

"Yeah."

I walk around the store slowly, searching for the perfect shirt to wear with the navy pants I purchased last weekend. White definitely works but is so blah. I finally decide on a lime green blouse with navy polka dots.

After I make my exchange and pay for the difference, I rush out of the mall to catch the next bus going my way.

I get home in time to have a light meal with the rest of

the family. Tameka's all dressed and ready, and so is Phillip. It won't take me long to shower and change. Auntie Mo and Chester will both be ready in a flash.

When Marcus and Randy show up at the house, I hold my breath, waiting to see how Auntie Mo is going to respond.

She hugs them both, which makes everyone happy.

"Is everybody ready?" Auntie Mo asks.

"I am," I respond. "And I have both cameras."

"Good," she says. "Let's go."

Marcus gives me a hug as we head out the front door. "What's up, little lady?"

"Well for one thing, I'm not a *little* lady. I'm almost grown."

He laughs. "Oh, really?"

"Yeah."

I ride with Tameka to the ceremony.

Auntie Mo cries all the way through the graduation. I don't know if she's crying tears of sadness or tears of joy that she's got one more out of her house. I know she loves us, but I'm so sure she's looking forward to coming home to an empty house.

I cheer for Traven when he strolls across the stage, looking all fine in that cap and gown. But when Brady's name is called, I shed a tear watching my brother walk across the stage to receive his diploma. I bet Mom and Aunt Cherise are shouting all over heaven right now.

I'm so proud of my brother.

Chapter 16

Auntie Mo is in military mode early Saturday morning. She has us get up at dawn to help her prepare for the barbeque. Auntie Mo and Traven's mom have been cooking for the past couple of days. Mr. Connor arrives promptly at 7:00 a.m. with a huge grill. Chester helps him set up in our backyard. I'm so glad Traven didn't come with his dad, because he would've seen me with this scarf on my head looking all tore up.

Then again, if he still wanted to get with me after that . . . it would have to be love he was feeling.

Tameka spent the night here with us so that she could help

Auntie Mo with the last of the cooking. They have me peeling potatoes for the potato salad.

I'm looking forward to the barbeque so that Traven and I can hang out, especially since Mimi is bringing Kyle. I already know she's gonna be all into him. With Traven here, I won't be left in the cold.

I just hope Kyle doesn't try to bring his boy with him. I don't want Gage to even know where I live. He's called my cell two or three times, but I haven't returned any of his calls. I'm not interested, and there's no point in pretending.

You can't buy my love.

Hmmm. I should use that as the title of one of my poems.

By the time twelve o'clock rolls around, we have the backyard decorated, the food cooked, and the picnic tables all set up. We take turns standing guard in the back while the others get dressed. Auntie Mo doesn't want to risk having anything out of place.

Tameka comes out to relieve me. "You can get dressed now," she says.

"Thanks. I'm glad you're here, because I have to run to the bathroom in a bad way."

She laughs. "Then you'd better hurry."

My first stop is the bathroom. Since I'm here, I jump into the shower. Afterward, I head to my room to take down my hair.

With Auntie Mo barking orders in between her cooking, everyone in the house is dressed and ready by one o'clock. The barbeque starts at two, but guests start arriving at one thirty.

Brady's girlfriend is the first to arrive. Shaquan cuts her eyes at me when he takes her by the hand to introduce her to a couple of people from our church. I still have a hard time believing that he's dating her.

Traven and Todd arrive minutes later.

"You look beautiful, Rhyann," Traven whispers in my ear.

"Thank you," I respond with a smile. I can't help but wonder what he would've said if he'd seen me earlier. "Everybody is out back."

Chester leaves to meet his brothers so they can pick up Brady's new car. But that's not the only surprise.

Tanya initially told us that she wouldn't be able to make Brady's graduation or the party, but right at 2:30 she strolls through the front doors, nearly scaring me to death.

"Girl, you took off some years of my life! I thought you weren't gonna be able to make it."

She hugs me. "I'm sorry, Rhyann. I wanted to surprise Brady. Where is that hard-headed boy anyway?"

"Did Auntie Mo know you were coming?" I ask.

Tanya shakes her head no. "I didn't tell anybody." She reaches back, holding her long hair off her neck. "Can I use one of your clips to put my hair up in a ponytail? The one that I had broke on the plane."

I rush to my room to get my cousin a ponytail holder.

"Here you are," I say, holding it out to Tanya. "Brady is out back with his girlfriend. He's going with Shaquan. You remember her?"

"That fast tail girl that used to live in the next block?

The one with all this here up here?" Tanya asks, gesturing.

I nod. "She still lives there and yeah—she has all that up there. Only now she's got some hips to match."

Tanya groans. "What is wrong with that boy?"

I shrug. "I don't know. He won't listen to me, but maybe you can get through to him. Did Auntie Mo tell you that Brady is going to USC on a full athletic scholarship?"

Tanya breaks into a grin. "Actually, Brady called me the same day he found out. He's so excited."

We stroll toward the back of the house.

"I'll let you walk out there first," I say.

She peeks outside. "Where is Chester and Randy?"

"They're picking up Brady's car before coming here. He doesn't know anything about it yet."

"Look at Mama," Tanya says. "She's just standing there looking all around. I think she's trying not to cry."

"I wish I could do something special for Auntie Mo. She's been so good to me and my brothers and Tameka."

"Marcus called me the other night. He wants to send her on a cruise this summer. He's just not sure she'll go."

"She doesn't want him spending drug money on her," I say.

Tanya gives me a sour look. "Marcus told me that he has a job and that's how he bought the tickets. He says that he's done with the dumb stuff. I believe him."

"I hope you're right. Auntie Mo is serious about this."

Auntie Mo does a praise dance when Tanya walks out of the house. "Thank you, Lord," she screams. "Praise Him for the great things He has done. Oh, thank you, Lord. Thank you."

Soon, Mimi and Kyle arrive. "Hey, what's going on?" she asks. "Is that Tanya?"

"Yeah," I respond. "She just got here. Tanya wanted to surprise all of us."

Kyle and Traven take a walk over to where Brady and some of the other guys are standing. I check out Mimi's cute pink-and-white halter sundress, her matching pink sandals and sunglasses. "Aren't you the diva? So where did you find that little outfit?"

"Girl, I bought this last summer but never wore it."

"It's nice. I like it."

"Did you get this from the store you were in yesterday?" Mimi asks, referring to my navy-and-khaki plaid Bermuda shorts and navy tube top.

"Sure did." I push my left foot forward to show off the navy blue flip-flops.

"I need some of those in that color."

"I bought them from Old Navy."

For some reason that reminds her of a question she wanted to ask. "Hey, are you still writing in your online journal?"

I nod. "Why?"

"I was thinking about starting one."

That takes me by surprise. "But I thought writing wasn't your thing?"

"Now that Kyle and I are together . . . I don't know. I guess he inspires me."

"Are you for real?"

"I'm falling in love with him."

I have an answer all ready for that, but I hold back. Instead I pick up two cups of lemonade and give one to Mimi. "You two haven't been together that long."

"So what?"

I embrace her. "Just be careful, Mimi. That's all that I'm saying."

"I hate when you get this way." She backs away from me. "Rhyann, I don't know why you're always so negative when it comes to boys, but it's getting old."

"I'm just being real, and I don't want to see you get hurt."

"Rhyann, I'm not rushing into anything, but I do know that I love him and I want to be with him in every way. I'm not telling you this for a lecture."

"Well, you're gonna get one anyway," I say. "We made a pact, Mimi."

"We were so immature when we did that. You and Dee may not be ready for intimacy, but what Kyle and I share is so strong."

Why didn't I see this coming? "I suppose he told you that he loves you?"

"Yes, he did actually."

I shake my head. "I can't believe you're falling for this."

Mimi takes my hand in hers. "Rhyann, I'm so sorry. I hate that you've been hurt so many times."

"Thanks a lot for making me sound all pathetic," I respond, snatching my hand away. "You're gonna lose some major B.F.F. points, Mimi. Just want you to know that. You might even lose a couple of Diva points."

Mimi chuckles. "You know I didn't mean it that way."

I'm not letting her off so easy. "People are always going to experience heartache from time to time. I've just gotten all of mine up-front. Hopefully, the next relationship will go smoothly."

"It will," Mimi assures me. "You already have the right guy." She glances over her shoulder to where the boys have all gathered. "Now Traven, he is crazy about you. Then there's always Gage. You know he was practically begging Kyle to bring him to the barbeque today."

"I'm so glad he didn't. Because I would've had to put them both out."

Kyle and Traven join us.

"The food looks good," Traven comments. "I'm throwing down in a minute."

"Me, too," Mimi says.

After my pastor gives the blessing over the food, we all get in line to fix our plates.

Brady comes over to me and whispers, "What's up with your girl Mimi? Why she bring that white boy to the barbeque?"

"The same reason you brought that white girl home last year. What was her name? Barbie . . ."

He laughs. "You wrong for that, sis."

"Mind your business, Brady. If you don't want anybody

talking about that thing you're dating, then don't talk about who anybody else is dating."

He's about to take offense, but then changes his mind. Leaning in close, he says, "I'm just gon' say this one thing to you—Rhyann, you need to give Traven a chance. He really cares about you." He backs off. "There, I'm done."

Chester and his brothers show up finally.

Auntie Mo gets everyone's attention and gives a brief tribute to Brady. She then hands a set of car keys to my brother.

"Are these mine?" he asks.

"No, Brady," I yell. "They're mine. They just want you to know what you'll be missing."

Mimi laughs. "Good one, Rhyann."

I shake my head at her in mock sadness. "Don't do that ever again. You just sounded like such a dork."

While we eat, Brady and Auntie Mo check out his new car, a used Ford Mustang.

Todd plays DJ for us after everyone has eaten the first round.

Traven's parents give tribute to him and present him with a gift.

Afterward, both Brady and Traven stand up to talk about how much they appreciate family.

I hug Brady when he's done. "Congratulations again, big brother."

Traven and I decide to walk around to the front of the house. He wants to spend some alone time with me. I look back to see where Mimi and Kyle are—they are still dancing.

Mimi's really happy when she's around him, and that's important to me. He'd better not break her heart.

"Have you given us some thought?" Traven asks.

We sit down on the front porch.

"I have," I say. "Traven, I like you and I'm not just talking about as a friend. I just think that you and I want different things in a relationship."

"What are you talking about, Rhyann?"

I hold out my left hand. "Do you see this ring on my finger?"

He is slightly startled. "Are you saying you want a ring?"

I chuckle. "No. Traven, this is a purity ring. I wear it because I made a vow to remain celibate until my wedding night. I intend to keep that vow."

Traven breaks into a smile.

"What are you grinning for?" I want to know.

"My church had a purity conference a couple of years ago and I took the same vow."

I don't bother to hide my surprise. "Then why were you trying to jump my bones prom night? I take my vow seriously."

It's Traven's turn to be surprised. "I didn't try to jump you, Rhyann."

"You didn't come right out with it, but you did say that we could do the same thing in the limo that could be done in a hotel. I'm not tripping—I heard you, Traven."

"I wasn't talking about sex. Rhyann, I know you're not like that. I just meant that we could still hang out and it didn't have to be in a hotel."

"Traven, I'm so sorry. I really thought you were trying to play me. I kept thinking about the girls you cheated on and that you just wanted to . . . you know."

"Rhyann, I'm not gonna lie to you. You fine and I have to do a whole lot of praying, but I'm committed to my vow just like you. It's hard . . . man, it's hard." Traven shakes his head. "Hey, I can't believe you brought up the cheating part. I was young and wild back then, trying to be like my big brother."

I laugh.

"I respect you, Rhyann. I'm not gonna pressure you into anything you don't want to do."

I give him a sidelong glance. "You're leaving for college in August. Do you really think a long-distance relationship is going to work?"

"I'd like to give it a try."

I look Traven straight in the eye. "One day at a time and we take it slow?"

He nods. "I'm okay with that."

"You're two years older than me, Traven. When you get to N.C. State, you might meet someone."

He's not convinced of that. "Rhyann, I'm sure she won't be as incredible as you." He takes my hand, holding it lightly. "I know that you're not ready to hear something like this from me, but I'm going to tell you anyway. I love you. I have for a long time and I know in my heart that you are the one for me. Until you can see that for yourself, I'm willing to wait."

I glance upward. *Lord, how am I supposed to respond to this?*

"I meant every word I've said," Traven states. "The ball is now in your court."

I lean toward him and plant my lips on his. They taste just as good as I'd hoped.

Mimi clears her throat noisily. "Um, we were wondering where you were. Are we, like, interrupting?"

Kyle takes her by the hand. "Maybe we should go check out the dessert table or something."

"You don't have to leave," I quickly interject. "Traven and I . . . we were just talking."

"Uh-huh . . . ," Mimi grunts.

"We have an announcement to make," I say, holding up our joined hands. "Traven and I are officially taking it one day at a time"—I pause for a heartbeat before adding—"as a couple."

"It's about time," Mimi screams.

Kyle smiles. "My man Gage is going to heartbroken, but that's cool."

Traven gives me a suspicious look. "Who is Gage?"

"Nobody you need to worry about," I tell Traven.

He and Kyle give Mimi and me some girl time.

"I'm so happy for you." She pulls out her cell phone. "I'm calling Dee right now so you can tell her the good news. She's going to be so happy for you."

I move to stop her. "Right now your happiness is about all I can stand, Mimi. I'll call her later on tonight. This is my news and I want to be the one to share it with her, okay?"

Mimi sticks her lips out in a pout. "Party pooper."

I have a boyfriend!

On Sunday, I'm still overflowing with happiness—not only because Traven and I are dating but also because Tanya's home and Auntie Mo has all of her children in church together. She's wanted this for a long time.

The moment I get out of Auntie Mo's van, I'm told, "Miss Christina wants to see you."

What does she want?

Miss Christina is one of two Temple of Praise dance leaders. She's not one of my favorite people right now, since Kelly won the spot. Still, I'm curious, so I head straight to the administration building.

"Morning, Miss Christina. You wanted to see me?" I say when I enter the choir room.

"Good morning, dear. Are you still interested in being on the praise team?"

I perk up instantly. "Yes, ma'am. Did another spot open up?"

"Kelly broke her leg last night, so she's going to be out for a few months."

"So you only need me temporarily then?" I ask.

Miss Christina shakes her head no. "One of the other girls will be leaving for college in the fall. You'll be replacing her."

I could hug Miss Christina right now. She is back among my favorites.

"Thanks so much," I say. "I won't let you down."

She smiles. "Rehearsal is Thursday night. Don't be late."

A new boyfriend and now a spot with Temple of Praise— life is wonderful!

Chapter 17

We arrive at church early so that I can meet with the other praise dancers. We learned a new routine, and our coordinator wants to make sure we have all of our steps on point.

I chat with a couple of the other dancers while we wait for Miss Christina to join us.

"Are you going with Traven Connor?" one of the girls asks me.

"Yeah," I respond cautiously. Please, no drama this soon in the relationship. I truly hope this chick is not about to tell me that she is interested in him. "Why?"

"I heard he took you to the prom."

"Yeah," I say. "Traven and I went to the prom together."

"His brother used to date my sister. She says Todd and Traven are really good people."

The grip on my feelings eases up a little. "Their whole family is nice."

"My sister says that his brother was her nicest boyfriend."

Miss Christina bursts into the room in a flash of violent fuchsia and yellow. "C'mon, ladies, we don't have much time."

She's the one who's late. Now she's trying to rush us around the place. Miss Christina needs to stop tripping.

We run through the routine a couple of times before she's satisfied. When we're done, we head over to the sanctuary to line up. This is my debut, and I'm beyond excited, because I love to dance.

Miss Christina is thinking of starting a dance team for the adults, but so far she hasn't found anyone willing to participate. I told Auntie Mo she should do it, but she laughs every time I mention it.

I'm dragging a little slow this morning because I stayed up late last night talking to Traven on the telephone. We have already figured out that we'll communicate via email, text messaging, and IM-ing when he goes away to college. Since he's going all the way to North Carolina, I won't be able to see him that much except during holidays, but at least we have the summer. I keep adding up the hours in my head. It's not going to be easy spending time with my girls and having quality time with my boyfriend in addition to working at the salon.

But I'm definitely up to the challenge.

After church, I head straight to my room to take a little nap.

When I wake up an hour later, I turn on my computer and log into my journal. I haven't written anything in a while.

June 1st

My brother Brady graduated on Friday night and he's going to USC in the fall. We gave him a barbeque on Saturday, and all of us had a blast. Tanya even came home to surprise us. She flew back to North Carolina early this morning because she has to work tomorrow. She must really love us to fly in for a few hours.

Traven and I are dating!!

I'm happy, but I'm also a little scared. He's going to be all the way in North Carolina, too, for college. What if he meets another girl there?

He told me that he loves me and I do believe him. At least I want to believe him—really, I do. But things happen—just look at Madison and Divine. She thought they would be together forever.

I'm a little more realistic, though.

I've known Traven for a long time and we are really good friends, so maybe things will turn out different for us because of that. Auntie Mo is always saying that you should be friends first in order to make a relationship work. I guess we'll see.

❦

"I thought Mrs. Goldberg had an appointment today," I say, checking the computer screen. "Did she change it?"

Miss Marilee shakes her head. "She's supposed to come in. She's probably just running late today. Ann is usually pretty good about calling me if she needs to cancel."

At Miss Marilee's request, I go up and get the next client.

"We're ready for you," I tell her.

I lead her back to the shampoo bowl, where I wrap the plastic cape around her to keep her from getting wet.

Every time someone walks through the front door, I glance up, expecting to see Mrs. Goldberg, but she never shows. This isn't like her at all to just not show up.

China calls in an order at the deli down the street. I offer to walk down and get it since I want to place an order for myself.

"You don't have to rush back," Miss Marilee tells me. "Sit down and eat, Rhyann. We can manage until you get back."

I glance over at China, who says, "That's fine. I'm not starving. Besides, I won't be able to eat until I'm finished with my client's hair."

I leave the salon, the earphones to my iPod in my ears.

In the deli, I order my sandwich and find a table near the window to sit while I wait for my food. One of the employees delivers it to me along with China's order. She gives me a soda on the house as I eat half my sandwich.

Traven's not working today, so I give him a call.

"What are you doing tonight?" he asks me.

"Nothing," I respond. "Why? What's up?"

"I thought that we could grab something to eat and then go to see a movie."

"That works for me," I reply. "Can you pick me up from work?"

"Sure. Same time?"

"Yeah." Our plans for the evening out of the way, we lapse into a real conversation. We discuss books we've read recently and our plans for the summer. Traven and I have a lot in common, and we get along so well that it's scary. I'm not waiting on the other shoe to drop, though. I'm planning to enjoy every minute I have with him.

No regrets.

"I can go to church with you on Sunday," Traven announces. "I told my boss that I needed that day off."

I smile. "That's great. You still have to go with me to Bible study, too. Remember, you promised."

He laughs. "I didn't *promise* that I'd go. I did say that I'd check it out."

"You better be glad I don't have time to argue with you. I'll see you at seven."

My break's almost over, so I sprint back to the salon to finish the rest of my workday.

When I walk outside again, Traven is waiting on me.

"How was your day?" he asks as we're driving down Sunset Boulevard.

"Fine," I respond.

He reaches over and takes my hand.

I'm so looking forward to our date this evening. I already know what I'm wearing tonight. I found this beautiful teal-and-purple dress that I'm going to wear over my skinny jeans. I have a pair of leather ballet slippers with teal and purple rhinestones that will go perfectly with my outfit.

I run my fingers through my hair, noting the need to get a retouch in another week. It's growing fast, and I can see that it's getting longer. I'm getting braids for the summer, so by fall my hair should be even longer. Not as long as it was, but I should be able to have a real decent ponytail, and not the Doberman pinscher one I've been wearing on bad hair days.

Traven drops me off at my house.

"Auntie Mo, can I go out with Traven tonight?" I ask as soon as I walk through the front door. "We're just planning to grab some burgers and then see a movie."

She smiles. "That's fine, sweetie. I'm going over to your sister's place so that she can do my hair."

"Just don't let Tameka put a pair of scissors in your head or trust her to do any color—you'll be fine."

"Rhyann, let it go, baby. Relax and release . . ." Auntie Mo advises. "C'mon. Relax and release."

Laughing, I trek off to my room, my heels making a steady rhythm across the hardwood floors.

I have a hot date tonight.

Chapter 18

When Ann Goldberg misses a second hair appointment a week later, Miss Marilee and I are both worried that something is wrong.

"So you haven't heard anything from Mrs. G?" I ask.

"I haven't," she responds. "I tried to call her earlier. I didn't get an answer, so I just left a message," Miss Marilee tells me. "I'll try her again in a few minutes."

She walks out to the reception area to pick up her client. After a brief meeting, she calls me over.

"Would you take Macy to the shampoo bowl, please? Use the Alterna White Truffle shampoo and conditioner."

I escort the client back while Miss Marilee walks over to a nearby telephone and begins dialing.

"This is Marilee at the Crowning Glory Hair Salon," I hear her say. "Mrs. Goldberg had an appointment today, and since she missed the one last week, too, I thought I'd call and check on her."

I wait anxiously for her to get off the phone. I hope Mrs. Goldberg is okay.

"I just spoke to Ann's husband," Miss Marilee announces. "She's not been feeling well."

"I had a feeling she was sick," I say. "I know how she is about that hair of hers. She likes to have it on point every week."

Miss Marilee agrees. "Her husband says that she should be here next week for her regular appointment."

"That's good. I'll pick her up some See's candies, since she's always bringing us some."

Miss Marilee smiles fondly at me. "I'm sure she's going to love that, Rhyann. You are such a thoughtful person. I love the basket of fruit you bought me yesterday."

Now I'm the one who smiles. "I know how much you like fruit, and people are always eating yours up, so I wanted to bring you some more. Besides, I was the one that ate up all the strawberries."

Miss Marilee chuckles. "Honey, it's okay. I don't just bring stuff in here for me. It's for all of us."

"I know you feed the homeless, too," I say. "Mimi told me that you even volunteer on Mondays at a homeless shelter."

"I want to help in any way I can," she responds. "Every now and then people just need to know that somebody cares about them."

I agree. "My aunt always says that we're supposed to give people their flowers while they can smell them. I didn't get it at first, but I do now. It's important to let people know how much you care about them while they're alive. It doesn't matter much once they die."

"You're really worried about that lady, aren't you?" Phillip asks when he comes into my bedroom. "I heard you talking to Auntie Mo about her."

"You need to stop listening to other folk's conversations." I pull two shirts out of my closet, trying to figure out which one to wear. I have Bible study in an hour.

"She's gonna be all'ight, Rhyann. I said a prayer for her."

I give Phillip a bear hug. "You are such a sweetheart. Thank you."

My phone rings. I smile when I see Traven's name on the caller ID.

"Hello."

"Hey, beautiful."

"What's up, Traven?"

"Nothing much. Just wanted to check on the girl of my dreams. I know you're going to your Bible study. Rhyann, I hope you know how much you mean to me. I really like spending time with you."

"Why is it you know exactly what I need to hear?" I ask. "I'm okay, but I found out that a friend of mine hasn't been feeling well. I'm worried about her. But anyway, how was your day?"

"It was okay," he responds. "Would've been better if I could've spent it with you."

"I feel the same way. However, we both had to work."

"I'm working the rest of this week, but I'm off Monday and Tuesday of next week. Do you have any plans?" Traven inquires.

A slight frown touches my lips. "My best friend is coming back, so we're sorta planning on hanging out."

"You're talking about Divine?"

"Yeah. You know that she and her cousin usually spend part of their summer vacation in Cali."

"That's why I used to hardly see you when school was out."

"Nope," I correct him. "You never saw me because you were usually working. You've been working from the time you started high school to now."

"That's true," he acknowledges with a chuckle. "I got to make that paper, you know."

"I understand," I say. "I have a job now, so I know it's gonna put a kink into my summer plans, but I need to start saving what I can for college."

"With your grades, I don't think you're gonna have any problems getting money for college."

"I hope not," I say.

"You won't," Traven reassures me. "Well, let's try and do

something Friday night, okay? I know you want to spend time with your girl, but we don't have much time before I have to leave for college."

"I know. Traven, we're gonna work this out."

"I'm not pressed. I waited this long for you."

I flash a grin. "I'm so worth it, Traven."

We receive a phone call from Mr. Goldberg a couple of days later.

I can tell from the part of the conversation I can hear that he's thanking Miss Marilee for the flowers we sent. At first she's all smiles, but when her expression changes, I feel deep in my gut that something's not right with Mrs. Goldberg.

"That won't be a problem at all," she says. "I'd be more than happy to come out to the house to wash and style Ann's hair. It might help her feel better."

Miss Marilee hangs up the phone, deeply concerned. "Ann is very sick. She's not well enough to come to the shop, so I'm going to make home visits on Saturday mornings."

"I want to go with you," I tell her. "She's my friend, and I'd like to see her." I'm trying to read the message on Miss Marilee's face, and it doesn't look good. "I know something is wrong with Mrs. Goldberg. I can feel it."

Her voice drops nearly to a whisper. "Rhyann, she has an inoperable tumor on her brain. Apparently she's had it for a while."

Her words hit me hard.

"Is she going to die?" The words pop out of my mouth before I can stop them.

"She's terminally ill," Miss Marilee responds quietly. "It's too far gone. Ann was never one for going to the doctor like she should. I told her to get herself checked out when she started complaining of headaches."

"I told her that, too, but Mrs. G said she didn't like going to the doctor. She said she always felt worse after seeing one."

Miss Marilee hugs me. "Don't worry, Rhyann. We are going to keep Ann lifted up in prayer. God can turn things around in an instant."

"I know, but there are times when He doesn't do a thing. He didn't save my mama." I pull away, feeling very sad. "I like Mrs. G. I don't want anything to happen to her." Tears roll down my cheeks. "I don't want her to die."

Miss Marilee gently wipes my face. "Why don't you go on home?"

I shake my head. "Miss Marilee, I have a job to do. I'm not gonna let my personal pain interfere with what I'm supposed to do here at the salon."

"I appreciate your professionalism, Rhyann."

"I'm going to get back to work," I say, seizing the idea. "Maybe if I stay busy . . ."

She nods in understanding.

"That's probably why she was having all those headaches and why she couldn't remember stuff."

"Most likely," Miss Marilee agrees. She starts for the door of the office.

"Can I be alone for a minute?" I ask. "I want to say a prayer for Mrs. G."

"Rhyann, take as much time as you need."

When Miss Marilee is gone, I raise my eyes upward. "Father God, I really have a big favor to ask. . . ."

Chapter 19

$\mathcal{S}$aturday morning, Miss Marilee picks me up and we drive to the Brentwood area, where Mrs. G lives.

Mr. Goldberg greets us warmly, then takes us upstairs to the master bedroom. This is my first time meeting him, but he acts like he's known me forever.

Even in her weakened state, with her complexion pale, her hair color fading, and her edges graying, an undeniable spark of light fills Ann Goldberg's eyes. "What a pleasant surprise. I'm so happy to see you and Marilee." She reaches up and touches her hair. "I guess my husband decided it was time to do something about this stuff on my head."

"Mrs. G," I say. "Your boo is really nice."

"Oh, is that what he is?" she asks. "I've been calling him a husband all this time. I didn't know I had a boo." She glances over at Miss Marilee and winks. "We perish for a lack of knowledge. You know, it used to have a different meaning when I was younger."

She can be so funny at times.

I head over to her bedside. "How are you feeling?" I can't believe how much weight she's lost. Mrs. Goldberg didn't have a lot of weight to start with. Despite her outward appearance, she's still so full of life, and she definitely hasn't lost her sense of humor.

"Well, ladies, I need you to make me fierce, as Rhyann likes to say. I want to keep my boo interested."

"Okay, Mrs. G. That's way too much information for me. Pull it back."

She laughs—not her usual throaty laugh but a laugh just the same.

"I've missed you, Mrs. G."

"I've missed you, too." She pats an empty spot on the bed. "Rhyann, come here and sit down. We have a lot of catching up to do. How are you and that boy . . . Traven, right?"

I break into a smile. "He and I are a couple now, but we're taking it really, really slow. He's leaving in August for N.C. State."

She gives my hand a gentle squeeze. "Good for you, dear. You're a very smart girl and you're going to make one heck of a lawyer one day."

"I hope so, Mrs. G."

"You will," she assures me. "I know so. I only wish I was going to be around to see it come to pass."

I feel a dull ache in the pit of my stomach. "Please don't talk like that, Mrs. G. You're going to—"

She cuts me off by saying, "Rhyann, it's okay. I'm ready."

I shake my head. "But I'm not ready for you to go anywhere, so you might as well get that thought out of your head. I like having you around."

"You're so sweet for saying that."

"I mean it. Mrs. G, don't you stop fighting. We need you here with us."

"That's what my mother told me earlier."

"You should listen to her."

Miss Marilee helps her sit up in bed so that we can use a no-rinse shampoo to wash her hair. I'd never heard of this until I started working at Crowning Glory. I couldn't imagine washing your hair without water, but it's pretty simple.

Miss Marilee applies the shampoo on Mrs. Goldberg's hair, working it through with her fingers. When it starts to foam, she tells me, "Now gently wipe it out, Rhyann."

When her hair is clean, Miss Marilee brushes it toward the back, where she makes a neat bun and secures it with hairpins.

Mrs. Goldberg gives me a smile, but it disappears as quickly as it came. I can see that she is getting tired. "I feel so much better," she says. "Thank you both."

"We're going to leave and let you get some rest," Miss Marilee tells her. "It's so good to see you, Ann."

I'm not ready to leave, but I know better than to argue. Besides, Mrs. G looks like she's already fallen asleep.

"I didn't expect to see her looking like that," I say when we are back in the car.

"I have to admit that her appearance threw me as well," Miss Marilee confesses. We pass the whole car ride in silence. When I get out, we both try to smile but fail miserably.

When I go inside, I find Auntie Mo in the family room with Tameka, who looks like she's been crying.

"What's up?" I ask.

"I just broke up with Roberto," she announces. "For good."

"Uh-huh," I remark skeptically. In a way, though, I'm glad to have this stupid drama. It takes my mind off the real tragedy.

"I mean it this time."

Both Auntie Mo and I look at her as if we've heard it all before.

"Some tramp came down to the school today looking for me," Tameka explains. "She tells me that she and Roberto have been together for five years and that they have three children together. Then she tells me that they're getting married. She even showed me a ring."

Talk about drama!

"I told you that man was no good," Auntie Mo says. "I had a feeling he had a family somewhere. I told you that he acts like a married man."

Tameka starts to cry.

Auntie Mo tries to comfort her.

I make sure my sister's okay before I head to my bedroom. I don't have any words of wisdom for Tameka. I don't really know what to say except kick the jerk to the curb and move on.

Traven arrives at seven to pick me up.

"I like the braids," he says as we head outside to his car.

"Thank you," I murmur when he opens the car door for me. Traven makes sure I'm secured inside before walking around to the driver's side.

"This is my summer hairstyle," I announce when he joins me in the car. "Since I plan on spending as much time as I can in a pool or on the beach, I wanted something low-maintenance."

"Speaking of the beach, my cousin is hosting a beach party next weekend. Do you and your friends want to go?"

"Yeah, we do. Are we gonna need tickets or anything?"

"I'll get you some invitations. How many do you need? It's two people per invite."

"Can I have three of them?" I ask.

"That's fine. I'll drop them off to you tomorrow evening."

When we reach the move theater, Traven parks the car and we get out. Lines are already beginning to form, so we walk briskly.

"This is the way it's supposed to be," he whispers while we are waiting to purchase our tickets. "The two of us together like this."

"I know," I respond, squeezing his hand tightly. "I feel the same way. This feels right."

I check my watch for the fifth time in a half hour. Divine and Alyssa's plane should be landing any moment, and I am so excited. I still don't get why Dee loves living in Georgia so much, but it doesn't matter—she's going to be here for the entire summer. We've already made plans to spend the coming weekend at Mimi's house.

"We're here," Divine announces when I answer my phone forty-five minutes later.

I break into a grin. "It's about time. Dee, where are you?"

"We're on the way to my house. I have to check in with Stella and get unpacked before Alyssa and I start hanging out. You know who is in Mom mode."

"I can hear you," I hear someone say in the background.

"Your mom is with you?" The last time I spoke to Divine, she told me that her mother was staying in Atlanta until July.

"Yeah," Divine responds. "She and Miss Emma decided to spend the summer out here with us. I think they have trust issues or something. I have no idea why."

"They probably don't want you running off to Vegas to get married," I say with a laugh.

"They definitely don't have to worry about that. Not yet, anyway," Divine says. "Hey, I have to get off the phone, but I'll see you in a couple of hours, okay?"

"See you then."

Three hours pass by the time Mimi's little red BMW pulls up in front of my house. Divine and I start screaming the moment we see each other.

"I can't believe you two," Mimi fusses. "You're so loud."

"Don't hate," Divine tells her. "I got some love for you, too."

Alyssa and I hug while Mimi and Divine compliment each other on their clothing.

"True divas," I observe.

"They sure are," Alyssa replies. "Fashion is Divine's middle name."

"Actually, it's Fashionista . . . don't hate . . ."

"I'm so glad you're here. Finally," Mimi states. "Rhyann has been so uncooperative."

"She's still mad because I didn't want to date *Mr. I'm so rich all the girls want to date me.*"

Alyssa chuckles while Divine inquires, "Who is that?"

"Gage Tenez. For some reason he really irritates Rhyann. He does talk about himself a lot, but I still like him." Mimi flips her hair over her shoulders. "I like Traven, too, and I do think that he's better for her. Not Gage."

"Well, you would like Gage, Mimi," Divine says. "The two of you have something in common. You both like to talk about yourself all of the time."

Mimi places her hands on her hips. "Oh, I know you not talking."

Alyssa and I crack up. Those two are too funny.

Chapter 20

$\mathcal{J}$erome and Ava's daughter just made her appearance into the world two hours ago. Divine and Alyssa are on their way to the hospital to see the baby. Although Divine is trying to act all nonchalant on the phone about everything, I can tell she's excited about having a baby sister. Divine's really been worried, but she tries hard not to show it. Maybe she thinks that she's being disloyal to her mother or something.

"How is your mom handling the news?" I ask.

"She's all right, I guess. You know she's all into planning her wedding right now."

"Is Miss Eula going with you and Alyssa to the hospital?" I ask. Miss Eula is their cook, but she's more like family. Divine told me that Miss Eula helped raise Jerome after his grandmother died. When Jerome and Miss Kara divorced, she got Miss Eula.

"No, she's going to visit Ava later this afternoon. She wants to buy a gift before she goes to the hospital. Stella's taking us there, and I think Mom's going to drop Miss Eula off on her way to a meeting."

"Are you planning on buying a gift?"

"I haven't really thought about it," Divine replies. "I guess I should, huh?"

"Probably," I say. "I know your dad would appreciate it—especially since he can't be with them."

"I'll pick up something from the hospital gift shop for now." Divine pauses for a moment before continuing. "We're going to Mimi's house afterward. Like around two. Are you coming by there? Mimi said she was going to call you."

"Yeah, but I already told Mimi that I won't get there until later," I state. "I have to go somewhere with Miss Marilee this morning."

"Oh, okay," Divine says. "Are you going to see a client?"

"Yeah. Mrs. G is sick. Remember, I told you about her."

"It must be serious if y'all are going to her house."

"She's real sick," I acknowledge. "Dee, she has a brain tumor and they can't operate."

"That sucks big-time."

"Tell me about it," I reply. "I'm scared she might die."

"Pray for her," Divine advises. "My uncle's always talking about how God can do anything. The thing is this—Rhyann, you have to believe. You know . . . have faith. Believe God for her healing."

"I am," I respond, feeling a twinge of hope. "You're so right. God can do all things, so healing Mrs. G ain't nothing."

I pray after Divine and I get off the phone. "Father God, I'm not trying to tell You how to run Your business, but Mrs. G—she needs You now. She needs healing, and only You can heal her. Please do this for me. If You do this for me, I won't ask for anything else."

Auntie Mo drops me off at Mimi's house before she heads over to the Cohens' estate for their summer barbeque. They have her working in the kitchen, but she doesn't mind, because they're paying her overtime. It's about time, as far as I'm concerned.

"How was your visit with Ava and your new little sister?" I inquire shortly after my arrival. "Is she cute?"

"She's adorable," Alyssa responds before Divine can open her mouth.

I glance over at my friend, waiting to hear what she has to say about the baby.

"She looks like Ava," Divine responds, holding up her camera phone. "I took some pictures. Her name is Sierra Michele."

"That's a pretty name." Mimi looks at the photos eagerly. "I like it. She doesn't really look like anybody to me."

"Ava says that Sierra has Divine's eyes," Alyssa blurts.

Shaking her head no, Divine utters, "She has Jerome's eyes."

"So do you."

"Whatever . . . ," she mutters. "Anyway, Sierra looks much better in person than in these pictures. She just hasn't found her photogenic side yet."

I laugh. "With a diva big sister, I'm sure she'll find her best side in no time at all."

Alyssa chuckles.

A few beats of silence pass before Mimi asks, "So how was it? What did you and Ava talk about?"

"Girl, you so nosy," I say.

"You want to know as much as I do," she counters, her eyes full of amusement.

"We talked mostly about the baby," Divine informs us. "Ava wishes Jerome could've been there. I can understand that. I can tell that she misses him a whole lot. She told me that she was so scared of losing the baby. She said that the cards I sent her when she was on bed rest kept her encouraged."

"Have you changed your mind about her?"

I pinch Mimi on the arm. "Stop being so doggone nosy."

"Rhyann, stay out of this," she demands. Rubbing her arm, she adds, "You are so not the boss of me."

"Mimi, that's so mature." I toss a pillow at her, which hits her square in the face.

Outraged, she snatches something from under her pillow and shoots me in the chest with it.

I glance down at my wet shirt. I can't believe what I see. "Really, Mimi—a water gun? You keep a loaded water gun under your pillow? What exactly do you think this is gonna do if someone breaks into your room?"

"Distract them until I pull out the knife in my drawer. And if that doesn't work, I'll just have to pull out my big gun."

I think she's bluffing. "I can't wait to see this. It's probably a butter knife from your mom's best silverware collection."

Alyssa and Divine fall back on the bed, laughing.

That's before Mimi opens her drawer and pulls out a huge hunting knife.

"Whoa! Put that thing away," I say, alarmed.

"Where did you get that?" Alyssa asks.

"My father gave it to me."

"So is the big gun a real gun?" Divine wants to know.

"No, guns are dangerous. It's a huge water gun. More like a water rifle, only I have water mixed with jalapeño juice, hot sauce, and black pepper in it."

"Okay, now I've heard it all," I say, trying not to laugh. "Here is the girl who doesn't mind spending thousands of her parents' money on unimportant stuff, and she's too cheap to buy some real pepper spray."

"It's illegal to have more than two ounces, I think, so I decided to make my own."

We look at each other and burst into another round of laughter.

"Hey, I don't want to be the one breaking the law," Mimi says.

"But Mimi, you don't think you'll get in trouble for making your own?" Alyssa asks.

"Well, the way I see it—if nobody comes into my room uninvited, I'll never have to worry about anyone finding my homemade pepper spray."

"You don't have any homemade bombs anywhere, do you?" I tease.

"No. I'm just sticking to the pepper spray."

She is so serious that we all break out laughing. Finally, Divine turns to me.

"I'm so glad your drought with boys is over."

"My drought?" I put my hands on my hips. "Oh no, you didn't go there. Just because it's been a while since I had a real boyfriend don't mean that I was in a drought."

"So what do you call it?" Divine asks.

Alyssa's cell phone rings.

She glances down at the caller ID and grins. "I'll be back in a minute. This is Stephen." Alyssa leaves the room for some privacy.

"I call it focusing on my studies," I tell Divine.

"Okay, that's the answer you give your parents, Rhyann," she says with a laugh. "What's the B.F.F. response? That's what we're waiting for."

I laugh too. "Okay, I admit that I might have been in a temporary slump. But I wouldn't say it was a drought. That implies an extended shortage of something—the key word being *extended*, like a long time. *Slump* simply means that there was a decrease or a decline."

"I guess Latin is really working out for you," Divine responds with a chuckle.

Mimi stretches and yawns. "Call it whatever you want, but it's been so long that I thought you'd retired from the dating game."

"I haven't retired—just wanted to wait until the right guy came along. That's all."

Divine winks. "As it turns out, he was always there."

"Girl, he was trying to knock my door down. I'm so glad I got a new doorbell."

Mimi frowns, not following. "What's your doorbell got to do with all this?"

"It's her way of saying she had a change of attitude, Mimi."

"Oh." She pulls out a small compact mirror and begins playing with her hair. "Can we please talk about me and Kyle now? I have loads to tell you."

Alyssa strolls into the room, asking, "Hey, did I miss anything good?"

"Mimi's about to brag about her wonderful relationship with Kyle and how much they adore each other," I say.

Divine adds, "And how she just knows he is the one for her."

"You two can be so mean," Mimi fusses. "You're just jealous of what I have with Kyle."

Divine and I look at each other. "Naaah . . . ," we say in unison.

"Well, anyway, Kyle and I do have a wonderful relationship. I *am* finding out that he can be a little moody. Some days he's really happy and upbeat, and then other times he's just so depressed. His father has been taking him to see a therapist . . ."

I fall back on the bed, groaning.

Mimi drones on and on. "But the thing is that we really do adore each other. I'm telling you, and you can laugh if you want. Kyle is the one for me. . . ."

"Why are you looking so sad?" Traven inquires as we head into Golf N' Stuff. "You used to like hanging out with me."

I take him by the hand. "Traven, I do like spending time with you. That is, until you open your mouth and ruin everything. All this trash talking you've been doing . . . You're still gonna lose."

He laughs. "Girl, you crazy."

I smile, but in fact I am feeling down, and Traven sees it.

He wraps an arm around me. "Okay, what's bothering you, Rhyann? You know that you can tell me anything."

We sit at an empty table. "There's this lady that comes to the hair salon—well, she's real sick. She has a brain tumor."

"Is she going to make it?" he asks, concerned.

I shrug. "I don't think so, Traven. Mrs. G is getting worse instead of better." I stop, thinking back on what I used to think about her. "I didn't like her when I first met her. I used to call her the red baron."

He laughs. "Why'd you call her that?"

"She has this bright red hair, she wore red lipstick, red nail polish, and she loves red shoes. Mrs. G says that red is her signature color. I used to think that all Jews were the same, but she is really a nice woman. Traven, she was the one who told me about the blacks in the concentration camps during the Holocaust."

"I didn't know that."

"I didn't, either, but I did some research and while there were not a lot, there was definitely some of us there."

"You really do care for her."

I nod. "I don't want to lose another person, Traven. I'm tired of people dying around me—people that I care about."

"I know what you mean," he replies. "My granddad and me. We were real close . . . when he died, I was so mad at him. He wasn't supposed to leave me. My mom told me that it wasn't his fault, though. He was just in the wrong place at the wrong time. So then I got mad at God."

"I think I was mad at God for a while, too. When my aunt died in Iraq . . . Traven, I thought I was gonna lose my mind. She and I were close."

"Remember at my granddad's funeral when I walked out?"

When I nod, Traven continues. "They were getting ready to do the prayer, and I wasn't ready to talk to God. I was too mad."

"I kind of did the same thing at my aunt's funeral," I confess.

"Are you still mad at God?" Traven asks.

I shake my head. "I don't know how I'll feel if something

happens to Mrs. G, though. It's too much." I meet his gaze. "What about you? Are you still angry?"

He pushes out his lips. "My granddad was in a lot of pain before he died, and I wouldn't have wanted him to live with all that. Hey, let's change the subject," he suggests, then kisses me on my forehead. "We're supposed to be having fun."

"You know what will make me happy right now?"

"What?"

I point over to the bumper cars. "Getting into one of those cars and racing you."

Traven laughs. "Rhyann, I'm telling you. It's not gonna happen."

"Watch me," I say.

He inclines his head. "That sounds like a challenge."

I break into a run, heading to the purple car while Traven jumps into a red one.

When it's time, I press the pedal in my bumper car and rush toward Traven's car, laughing the whole time.

"My car won't move," he yells.

"You actually have to step on the pedal."

"I know that," he shouts back. "The car won't move."

I back up away from him.

In a surprise move, he plows into me.

"You're such a liar," I say.

"Stop whining."

"If it's a fight you want," I cry, "then it's a fight you're gonna get."

When I get home four hours later, Auntie Mo meets me at the door, wanting to know every single detail of my date with Traven.

Talk about nosy.

"Did you have fun?" she asks.

"Yes, ma'am," I respond. "We went to Golf N' Stuff. We played miniature golf and rode in the bumper cars. You know how much I like them. We had so much fun."

She notices how happy I am, and she coughs uneasily. "Have you considered what will happen when Traven leaves for college?"

"I'm trying not to think about it right now, Auntie Mo. I just want to enjoy the time we have together."

"I like Traven a lot, and I think he's good for you. I just don't want to see you become so serious about him."

"We're taking it slow, Auntie Mo. You don't have to worry."

She hugs me. "I don't want to see you hurt. It breaks my heart to see my children in pain. But you're using your head, so I feel much better. Now go on to your room. I know you're dying to call Mimi and Divine."

Auntie Mo knows me too well.

"I'll see you in the morning," I say.

"Don't stay on that phone all night, Rhyann. You have to get up early tomorrow."

"For what?" I ask.

"Your dentist appointment," she answers. "I told you about it last week."

"I forgot," I reply. "But I'll be up in time."

I get Mimi and Divine on three-way as soon as I settle down in the middle of my bed. Alyssa picks up an extension phone so that we can all talk as if we were in the same room.

"How was your date with Traven?" Divine inquires. "You have fun?"

"We had a lot of fun," I say.

"Well, spill," Mimi demands. "Don't keep us hanging. Hey, is he a good kisser?"

I laugh. "You're so nosy."

"We all want to know," Divine interjects. "So you might as well answer the question."

"Yeah," I say. "He's a real good kisser. I'm gonna miss him so much when he leaves in August. I hate even thinking about it. I was doing pretty well until my aunt mentioned it earlier."

"He'll be home before you know it," Divine tells me.

"Yeah," I murmur. "Anyway, I'm not gonna focus on that right now. So tell me, what did you all end up doing? I know you missed me."

Mrs. G's condition has worsened, and she's unable to get out of bed or even sit up for long periods of time. I just found out that she's been put under hospice care, which makes me feel really sad. I don't want to upset her, so I try to hide my emotions whenever we go to the house.

Miss Marilee pulls me off to the side. "Rhyann, we can't

walk into that room with tears in our eyes. Wipe your face."

"I'm sorry."

"Hon, I know how hard this is on you. Maybe it's not such a good idea for you to come."

"No, Miss Marilee," I quickly protest. "I don't know how much time she has left, and I want to spend some of it with her."

"Okay, but put a smile on that beautiful face of yours."

Miss Marilee has to wipe away her own tears before we enter the bedroom.

"My two fav . . . favorite girls . . . ," Mrs. Goldberg mumbles when she sees us. "Come to make me gorgeous." She tries to sit up.

I rush to her bedside. "Take it easy, Mrs. G. You can just lay right there. We got you. You know we got skills."

"M-mad skills . . ."

Mrs. Goldberg can still make me laugh, but I can't shake the feeling that this might be the last time I see her.

"Rhyann, I want you to do something for me," she says right before we get ready to leave.

"Sure," I respond. "What do you need, Mrs. G?"

"It's not for me, dear. It's for you. I want you to live each day to the fullest. Live as if every day is your last. Don't grow up with a single ounce of regret." She places her hand over her heart. "I'm not sad to have to leave this world, because I have no regrets. I enjoyed my life—I really did. Now, will you do that for me?"

I struggle to keep my tears from falling. "I will, Mrs. G. I promise."

She reaches up to wipe away an escaping tear from my eye. "Don't cry, sweetheart. This is not what you want for me." She winces, and her face seems gray. "I am lying here in so much pain. I'm fine when they give me medication, but otherwise, the agony is too much to bear at times. I don't have a strong constitution for pain."

"No, ma'am. I don't want you in all that pain. But—"

Mrs. Goldberg interrupts me. "I'm ready to leave this world, Rhyann. And when I go, I will carry you in my heart."

I take her pale ivory hand in my chocolate-hued one. "Thank you for being my friend, Mrs. G. You taught me so much, and I want you to know that I'll never forget you. I wish I could've had more time with you."

"If I'd ever had a daughter . . . I would want her to be just like you, Rhyann. Of course, I'd have to do some explaining to my boo."

I laugh, but it's cut short when she grimaces.

"Are you in pain?" I ask.

She nods limply.

Miss Marilee goes to the door and asks the nurse to come.

"I'm never going to see her again, am I?" I ask Miss Marilee when we leave the bedroom. "She's so weak."

She hugs me. "I don't know, sweetie. All I know is that we're going to miss her so much."

Just as we walk outside, Mrs. Goldberg's mother arrives.

"Mrs. Braddock, it's nice to see you," I say.

She greets me with a hug. "Thank you for coming. You and Marilee. I know Ann appreciates it greatly. She's always cared about her appearance."

"How are you holding up?" Miss Marilee asks.

"As well as I can. This is so hard for me. I've seen so much death . . ."

"I feel the same way," I say. "Life really isn't fair."

"No, it isn't," Mrs. Braddock agrees. "But we live on, trying to make it just one more day. My Ann . . . I don't want to lose her, but it pains me even more to see her wasting away in that bed upstairs."

I'm totally surprised when Mimi, Divine, and Alyssa show up at my house that evening.

"What are you guys doing?" I ask. "Slumming?"

"No," Mimi responds. "This is a nice area. It's not a slum."

I glance at Divine, and we break into laughter. Mimi can be such an airhead at times.

"What's so funny?"

"Nothing, Mimi," I respond.

We all pile into my not-huge bedroom.

"I see you and Divine have the same passion for purple," Alyssa says.

"You just changed your room from that Pepto-Bismol pink to a black-and-white theme," responds Divine.

"With red accents," Alyssa interjects with a smile. "I want a room that shows my maturity."

"Like whatever," Divine mutters.

When her cell phone starts ringing, Divine checks the caller ID. She looks puzzled. "It's T. J. I just talked to him last night."

"Your boo is missing you," Mimi teases.

"I'll call him back later. I'm kicking it with my B.F.F.'s right now."

Alyssa laughs. "She'll be calling him back in about five minutes. Just watch."

Divine elbows her. "I'm not like you. I don't have to talk to T. J. every other hour. I'm surprised your phone isn't blowing up already. Stephen is usually so prompt, and look, he's already missed the noon call."

"Ha-ha . . . so funny," Alyssa mutters. "Don't hate . . . my boo loves hearing my voice."

"Rhyann, what's wrong?" Divine asks. "You seem like you're in your own little world."

"I was just thinking about Mrs. G. She's getting worse . . . she's going to die. I prayed so hard for her. I thought she would be healed—that's what I prayed for."

"Nooo . . . ," Mimi says. "That's so sad."

"She looked so weak when I saw her earlier. I keep praying for God to heal her, but I don't think he's hearing me."

"He is," Alyssa assures me. "God hears all of your prayers."

"Alyssa is a preacher's kid," Mimi says. "Maybe she should pray for Mrs. G."

"Being a PK doesn't give Alyssa a direct hotline to God," Divine interjects.

"But it might give her bonus points," Mimi says with a chuckle. "We don't go to church at all, but when I get to heaven, I'm going to tell God that it's my parents' fault."

"Why don't you go without them?" Alyssa suggests. "You don't have to wait on your parents to take you. You drove all the way here and we passed quite a few churches along the way. Just pick one and go."

"Is God going to hold it against me if I don't go?" she wants to know.

"Mimi, God's not like that," Alyssa states. "He'll meet you wherever you are. You only have to open your heart, repent of your sins, believe with your heart, and confess with your mouth that Jesus Christ died on the cross and rose from the dead so that you might be forgiven and have eternal life in the Kingdom of Heaven. Then you will receive the gift of Salvation."

Shaking her head, Mimi says, "No, that's like way too easy. It's got to be more than that, because if it were that easy, why isn't everybody saved?"

"Because some people don't have a lot of faith and they listen to what the world is saying," Alyssa responds. "That's why it's so important to read the Bible and get to know Jesus for yourself."

"It still sounds too easy to me," Mimi says. "There has to be more to it."

"There is," Divine confirms. "You have to find a church

home and like Alyssa says, read the Bible. You love drama, so you shouldn't have a problem with the Word. There's a whole lot of drama in the Bible."

I nod in agreement, but my heart is filled with sadness over the thought of Mrs. Goldberg dying.

You didn't save my mom or my aunt. Why won't you at least save my friend, God?

Chapter 21

Miss Marilee meets me at the door when I walk into the salon four days later. We head straight back to her office. I notice that everyone is pretty quiet.

She looks upset about something, so I ask, "Did I do something wrong?"

"No, hon," she responds. "Not at all. The reason I brought you back here is because I need to tell you something."

Scanning her face, I can tell Miss Marilee's been crying. "What's wrong?"

"Ann Goldberg died early this morning."

Shocked, I put a hand to my mouth. "But we just saw her

on Saturday. She didn't look like she was gonna die so quickly." I think back, remembering her looking so frail in that bed. "I know she said she was ready. I guess God took her up on it."

"Her husband called me shortly after I got here. He said she passed peacefully."

"How is he doing?" I ask, trying to hold back my tears. "And Mrs. Braddock? Is she okay?"

"He's as well as can be expected, I guess," Miss Marilee responds. "Her mother is taking it pretty hard, though. She had to be hospitalized this morning."

I place my hand across my stomach, trying to calm the nervousness inside. "I knew it was gonna happen, but I still can't believe this."

"It's still hard for me to grasp as well," Miss Marilee echoes. "Rhyann, you should go on home. I know how much you liked Ann, and I know it's hard on you. China's leaving in a few minutes—she can take you home."

I don't argue with Miss Marilee this time. I'm definitely not in the mood to work today. Besides, I can't keep my tears back any longer.

I stay in the office until China comes to the door, saying, "I'm ready. We can leave now."

Auntie Mo is waiting on the porch for me when I get home. Miss Marilee must have called her and told her about Mrs. Goldberg. She doesn't say a word, just holds out her arms to me.

I rush into them, seeking her comfort.

My tears fall at once. "She's g-gone," I moan.

"I know, baby. I'm so sorry."

"I don't u-understand, Auntie Mo. Why did God take her?"

"I don't know. Maybe He needed her with Him."

"He's God," I say. "He doesn't need anyone."

"Ssssh . . . sweetheart. Let's go into the house."

Auntie Mo takes me to the kitchen and fixes me a cup of hot chamomile tea. I cry until no more tears will come.

"Why don't you go lay down for a while?" she suggests.

I nod and make my way to my bedroom.

Divine calls me around six, waking me up. "Where are you? Are you with a client?"

"I'm home," I respond.

"Oh, I thought you were working today," she says.

I sit up in bed. "I went to work, but I had to leave. I couldn't work today because of some bad news."

"What happened?" she asks.

"My friend is dead," I announce. "Mrs. G is dead."

"Oh, I'm so sorry, Rhyann. Do you want us to come over?"

"To be honest, Dee, I just want to be alone. I'm still having trouble believing it."

"I'm not trying to be cruel or anything, but you sorta knew this was going to happen."

"I really didn't think it would be this soon, Dee. I just saw her on Saturday. Yeah, she looked weak and all, but I really thought she had more time."

A hot tear rolls down my cheek. "This is so wrong. Her dying just reminds me of my mom's death and then losing Aunt Cherise. Right now I'm so mad at God. I can't even talk to Him right now."

"I wish there was something I could say to make you feel better."

"I wish you could tell me why my mom and my aunt had to die. Why did Mrs. G have to die?"

Nothing but silence fills the other end of the phone.

"Are you going to the funeral?" Divine asks, after a brief pause.

"Yeah. I think she'd want me there."

"I'm really sorry, Rhyann."

"Me too."

"You sure you don't want us to come over? We don't have to stay long, but I just think we need to be there for you."

I try to muster up a joke. "You can come only if you all agree to not take any pictures of me with my swollen eyes. I look like a frog right now."

"We'll give you a reprieve this time, Rhyann. Do you want any comfort food?"

"Auntie Mo is making macaroni and cheese for me. Can you bring me some chocolate ice cream?"

"Sure. Anything else?"

"Something funny to watch," I say. "Make sure it has nothing to do with anybody dying. I can't handle another death."

"Okay, I have my orders. You get some rest and we'll be there soon."

"Thanks, Divine."

"You've always been there for me. This is the least I can do for one of my B.F.F.s. See you in a few."

"Okay."

Mimi, Divine, and Alyssa show up with pepperoni pizza, ice cream, popcorn, and movies two hours later.

"Wow . . . ," I murmur.

"We're here to cheer you up," Mimi states with her *I'm so happy* attitude. Right now I find that a bit irritating.

"I'm not sure your plan is gonna work," I respond. "I'm so not in the mood to be cheered up." My eyes travel to Divine. "Sorry. I told you this might not work."

She hugs me. "That's why we're here. If you need to cry— do it. I'll pass the tissues."

"Where do you want me to put this pizza?" Alyssa asks.

Auntie Mo strolls into the living room. "Hon, I'll take it and put it on the counter. How have you been, Alyssa?"

She smiles. "Fine, Miss Winfield. Glad to be out of school for the summer."

"Look at you, Divine. You're growing up into a fine young lady."

I make a face.

"Don't hate . . . ," Divine whispers.

After a moment, I say, "I did what you told me to do, Dee. I prayed for her and I believed that she was going to be healed. Maybe it's because I'm not doing something right."

"It's not you, Rhyann," Alyssa tells me. "My daddy preached about this a couple of weeks ago. He told me that there were two types of healing. Healing on this side and healing on the other side. Your friend is healed—she's not in any pain now."

"I guess I hadn't looked at it like that," I mumble. "I would rather have her healed and living in this world. I know it sounds selfish, but it's the truth."

"You'll see her again," Alyssa says.

"Rhyann hopes she will, anyway."

I resist the urge to snatch that weave out of Mimi's head. "You're the one who has to worry if Jesus is gonna slam the door in your face. I go to church, so He's seen me many times. He doesn't have a clue as to who you are."

Deep down I know that's not true. Jesus knows all of us, including people who deny Him. I just like irritating Mimi from time to time.

"I'm going to heaven, too," she counters. "I did what Alyssa told me to do. I did it when I went home that night. You all won't be getting rid of me that easy. I'll be right up there with you. *So there.*"

We can't help but laugh. That chick is a nut, but I love her.

China does some research on Jewish funerals and gives her mom and me a quick tutorial on some of the customs. "When someone dies, the body is never left alone," she states.

"What do you mean, it's never left alone?" I ask. "Who in

their right mind would want to stay around a dead body?"

"It's their way of honoring the dead," China explains. "The guardian prays for the soul and reads psalms from the time of death to the burial."

"Our funerals are nothing like that," I comment. "You wouldn't be able to get not one person in my family to sit with a dead body. We'll pray for your soul, but we won't be sitting beside your body like that. No way."

"Oh, the other thing is that we can't wear pants. The women wear dresses to the funeral."

"I can do that," I say.

"And we should try to get there early. From what I read, Jewish funerals start on time."

Both Miss Marilee and China glance in my direction.

"I'll be on time," I say.

The next day, I ride with Miss Marilee and China to the funeral.

"Do I look okay?" I whisper to China.

She nods in approval at my navy blue dress and matching shoes. "You look perfect. Mrs. G would be so pleased."

"She'd probably think I'd lost my mind. You know how flashy she used to dress."

"You're probably right," Miss Marilee says in a low voice.

When we arrive, the funeral director directs us to our seats after giving each of us an attendance card to fill out. I notice that Miss Marilee adds a brief message of condolence, so I do the same.

I glance around the funeral parlor. Mrs. Goldberg had

many friends, from the looks of it. As people filter in, a low rumble of conversation develops.

The family enters. I notice how pale Mrs. Braddock looks, and I say a silent prayer that she'll be strong enough to get through this day.

The rabbi leads the congregation in prayer.

My eyes fill and overflow during the eulogy.

After the service, I walk out to the car with China and Miss Marilee.

China places the sticker on the windshield, identifying her car as part of the funeral.

"I'm going to miss her," Miss Marilee says once we're in the car and on our way to the cemetery.

"Me too," I say from the backseat. "That little redheaded diva turned out to be a pretty nice person."

China chuckles. "I remember the first time I met Mrs. G. That woman knows she worked my nerves. I told Mama that we should've just limited our clientele to African Americans. But the more I got to know her, the more I liked her, even though she wouldn't leave a tip for nothing. Mama was the only one willing to do her hair."

We reach the cemetery fifteen minutes later, and we are directed to the graveside, where we find rows of empty chairs for the family. Just as I'm about to drop down into one on the last row, China whispers, "These are for the family and close friends, Rhyann. We're supposed to stand around the grave."

"Oh," I mutter.

After several very long prayers, it's a struggle to maintain my attention until the end of the service, when we're invited to throw dirt into the grave after the casket is lowered.

After the funeral, Mr. Goldberg comes over to us. "Thank you all for coming."

"Ann was a dear friend," Miss Marilee tells him. "I wouldn't be anywhere else."

"Ann left a letter for you, Rhyann. I'll have someone drop it off at the salon in a few days."

"Mr. Goldberg, I understand. Take your time." I want to make anything I can easy for him. "If I'm not there, I know Miss Marilee will make sure I get it."

He smiles. "I can see why my Ann loved all of you so much."

"We loved her, too," China responds.

Mrs. Braddock greets us with tears in her eyes. We speak with her for a few minutes, then take our leave.

By the time I make it home, I'm mentally exhausted.

Traven comes by to check on me, and we end up watching a movie together with Brady and Phillip.

After Traven leaves, I go to my room.

I turn on my computer and log into my journal.

July 2nd

I attended Mrs. G's funeral earlier today. I'd never been to a Jewish funeral before. If it hadn't been my friend's service—I could probably appreciate this more but instead my heart hurts.

It hurts because I miss her. Mrs. G was sweet, funny and a snazzy dresser—at least that's how she described herself. Her husband—no, her boo—told me that she left a letter for me. I don't know what it says or when I'll read it. I just don't think I can do it anytime soon. Maybe when the pain isn't so bad.

I didn't get to say everything I wanted to say to her. There wasn't enough time, so I guess I'll do it here:

Mrs. G:
I hope that you aren't in any pain anymore now that you're gone. I'm still kinda hot about your leaving, but I didn't want you living in all that pain. You are very brave, and I hope that I will have that kind of courage when it's my time to meet death.

I wasn't feeling you when we first met because I considered you just another Jew with an attitude, but I had it twisted. I was the one with the attitude. You showed me that. You taught me that I have to look beyond the skin to see the heart. Thank you for that.

I'll never forget you.

Chapter 22

When I stroll into the salon the Tuesday after the Fourth of July, Miss Marilee hands me a white envelope.

"What's this?" I ask. "Miss Marilee, are you giving me my walking papers?"

She laughs. "Samuel Goldberg sent this over by messenger. He also dropped off these."

I take the canister of toffee-ettes from her with a smile. "That Mrs. G. I know she had him do this."

"Aren't you going to read your letter?" China asks.

"I don't know. I don't think I'm ready."

Miss Marilee gives me an understanding nod.

I hold the envelope out to her. "Would you do it, please?"

"Are you sure, Rhyann?"

"I want you to read it."

Miss Marilee opens the letter and reads. Her eyes keep widening until she glances up at me. "Rhyann, I think you should read this yourself."

I'm puzzled by her reaction. "Why? What's wrong?"

The entire hair salon has suddenly grown quiet.

I take the letter from Miss Marilee.

> *My Dear Rhyann:*
>
> *Life is all about seasons. And for this short season of my life, I want you to know that you have been a sprig of hope for the future. Despite very humble beginnings, you continue to strive for excellence in your studies, and I admire your work ethic. You've designed a course for your life and set realistic goals—all of which should be rewarded.*
>
> *At my request, my husband has set up a fund that will pay for your education, including books, at the college or university of your choice. I don't want you to have to worry about financing your education any longer. I fear it may distract or discourage you from your studies. However, should you choose not to attend college in the future, please understand that no monies will be forthcoming. Have your aunt get in touch with my boo, and he will take care of everything on his end.*

You were a gift to me, and this is our gift to you—our sprig of hope for the future.

Ann

My knees buckle, and if Miss Marilee hadn't been standing here to catch me, I probably would've hit the floor. "Omigosh! OMIGOSH!" I scream. "Oh, Miss Marilee, I'm so sorry. I didn't mean to yell like that, but I'm going to college." I get more excited the more I talk. "I'm going to be able to go to college and not sell my brother's firstborn child because I'm not having any."

Everyone in the salon starts clapping.

Miss Marilee hugs me. "God is good."

"Yes, He is," I murmur softly, tears streaming down my face. I'm losing so many diva points right now, but I don't care.

I look up at the ceiling and whisper, "Thank you, God, and thank you, Mrs. G."

I ride with Divine and Alyssa to her stepmother's house in Baldwin Hills. We're going to see the baby and present our gifts. This is like the fourth or fifth present Divine's taken her baby sister. She still hasn't admitted it yet that she's crazy about that little girl.

"Sierra's getting so big," Alyssa comments while we're in the back of the Lincoln Town Car.

Divine doesn't say anything because she's too busy texting someone on her cell phone.

Alyssa grins. "Must be T. J."

"Like you haven't been on the phone most of the morning with Stephen," Divine responds, not looking up. "T. J. says he misses me."

"Awww . . . ," I say.

"When was the last time you talked to Traven?" she asks me.

"Last night," I respond. "But we're not on the phone all day and half the night like you and T. J."

"That's because your boo has a job. T. J. is working now, but he can talk to me while he's at work."

"Don't get that boy fired," I tell Divine. "That would be ugly, you know. Especially when you have to pay for everything."

Divine considers my words, then nods. "Girl, you're right. T. J. needs that J-O-B."

Our driver pulls into the circular driveway of Ava's home and rolls the car to a stop. We all pile out.

"Are you sure Ava doesn't mind all of us being here?" I ask.

"It's a fine time to ask now," Divine responds. "You're already here, but no, she told me that you guys could come."

"Hi, Mrs. Hardison," I say when she opens the front door. "Congratulations on the baby."

Ava moves to the side to let us enter. "You're welcome, Rhyann. It's nice to see you again."

"Are you okay?" Divine asks, surveying her from head to toe.

Even I can see how pale she looks, and the dark circles

under her eyes make her look ages older. Girlfriend could definitely use some concealer right about now.

She nods. "Just tired. The baby sleeps all day long and is up at night."

"My brother's baby was like that when he was first born," Alyssa offers. "My parents said that you have to turn them around. Keep Sierra up during the day, or you sleep when she sleeps."

Nodding, Ava responds, "I think I read that somewhere. I have so much to do—laundry, making bottles—it's a challenge just to get in a good shower. I had no idea how exhausting this could be."

"Ava, what do you need us to do while we're here?" Divine asks. "You can go get in bed and we can help out with whatever you need."

Ava's clearly surprised by Divine's proposal. I think we all are, to be honest.

"Divine, you're so sweet, but you don't have to do anything."

"Yeah, I do," she counters. "I don't mean no harm, but, Ava, you look like you're about to pass out. Let us help you. I can feed Sierra when she wakes up. You have milk in bottles, right?"

Ava grins. "I pumped some not too long ago."

Divine frowns. "That sounds gross."

I give her a playful pinch on the arm. "Stop . . ."

Mimi pulls out a pen and a small notebook. "Do you need anything from the store? Alyssa and I can take care of that."

While Ava gives her a list of items, Divine leans toward me and whispers, "I knew Mimi was going to find a way to get out of doing any cleaning or laundry."

"She doesn't clean up at home. You know she's not gonna do it anywhere else," I respond in a low voice.

"Forget both of you," Mimi states. "I know you're talking about me."

Alyssa chuckles. "Y'all are too funny."

Divine takes care of the baby while Ava is in her room taking a much needed nap. I move about the room, picking up magazines and dusting. After Sierra is changed and fed, Divine and I finish the laundry. We both balk at cleaning the bathrooms, so we leave that for Alyssa, since Divine says that she's the Bathroom Queen.

After Alyssa and Mimi return, Divine goes to check on Ava.

"How are things going with you?" Alyssa asks me.

"I'm getting better. I get the healing on the other side part—really I do, but I just miss her, you know. I still look for Mrs. G every Tuesday at four."

"It's gonna take some time, Rhyann," Alyssa assures me. "But that's so sweet what she did for you."

I smile. "It really is. I'm so excited now about college."

Divine comes out of Ava's bedroom and announces, "I'm going to stay here for the rest of the week to help with the baby. I've already called my mom, so I won't be going back with y'all. Alyssa, you can stay here, or Mom said you can come back to the house."

"I'll stay here with you," she says. "Is Ava okay?"

Divine nods. "She's tired, and she feels really alone with Jerome away." Her gaze travels to my face. "Don't even say it," she warns. "This is just a day-by-day kind of thing."

Traven and I drive to Santa Monica, where we are planning to hook up with Mimi, Kyle, Alyssa, and Divine. Since the outing is more of a couples thing, Alyssa and Divine are bringing two friends from school. Daniel and Chris already know the deal with Alyssa and Divine, so they are not trying to hit on them.

"Your friends are pretty cool," Traven tells me. "I like that you all really care about each other."

"Yeah, we're all really close."

"How are you doing?" he asks me.

"I'm getting better, I guess. I really miss Mrs. G. Sometimes I still look for her to come into the salon."

"That's so great about the college fund. She really liked you, Rhyann. And she knew how much you wanted to go to college. I mean, anyone who'll actually try to make money stuffing envelopes or selling crappy stuff over the internet . . ."

"You would bring that up," I say.

"I'm just saying. You know what you want, and you go after it—I think that's pretty cool."

I smile at his compliment.

"Rhyann, have you thought about which college you want to attend?" Divine asks.

"I'd like to go to Spelman," I answer, reaching for Traven's hand. "Atlanta isn't that far from North Carolina."

"Cool," Divine says, pleased. "That's where Alyssa and I want to go."

"What about you, Mimi?" Alyssa inquires.

"Well, I guess if all of you are going to Spelman, then I should go there, too."

"You don't have to," Alyssa says. "You can go anywhere you want to go. It's college."

"But I would rather be with my girls. You may not know this, but I don't get along with a lot of people—girls especially. They're always so jealous of me."

I laugh. "Then you really don't want to go to Spelman. It's an all-girls school."

"I know that, but if you all can do—so can I," Mimi states. "That settles it. We're going to Spelman."

I really enjoy hanging out with my friends. We don't always agree, but when it matters most, I know that Divine, Mimi, and Alyssa have my back. Auntie Mo says that's what it means to really be a friend.

Readers Club Guide for

it's a *Curl* thing

by Jacquelin Thomas

SUMMARY

Rhyann Hamilton has big plans: to make top grades, get a scholarship to her dream college, and have a great time at her sophomore prom. But after a hair disaster leaves her owing money to a local hair salon, she finds herself in a new role, tending to pampered customers as an assistant at the salon. There she meets a new friend who challenges her to think differently about the world and her own place in it. With the help of her friends Mimi and Divine, Rhyann learns that when she reaches out to others, opens up, and trusts in God, her world expands in ways she'd never imagined.

Questions for Discussion

1. What is your first impression of Rhyann? How does she differ from her friends Mimi and Divine? What do you think are her character strengths and weaknesses? How does she change over the course of the story?

2. Right from the beginning of *It's a Curl Thing,* Rhyann is focused on how her hair looks—and horrified when her sister bungles her cut and color. Why do you think hairstyle and appearance are so important, not just to Rhyann and her friends, but also to Mrs. Goldberg? Can you relate?

3. Why do you think Rhyann resists trusting Traven? Do you think she's heard too much about his past, or does she tend to distrust all men? Is she right to be hesitant about him, or has she let her prejudgments cloud her view of him? Why do you think her true feelings only come out in her poems?

4. How does Rhyann blind herself to her own anti-Semitism? How does she let her aunt's experience feed into it? How does her anger create a false impression of Mrs. Goldberg? What do you think really wakes up Rhyann to her own prejudice?

5. After her confrontation with Mrs. Goldberg, Rhyann realizes that in order to get respect you have to earn it. Do

you agree that respect is something that must be earned? How does Rhyann step up and earn respect at the salon?

6. Rhyann and Divine are both surprised to learn that there were black victims of the Holocaust. Was this new information for you as well? Why do you think certain aspects of history might not be taught in school?

7. Unlike Divine and Mimi, Rhyann doesn't come from a privileged background. How does this affect her opinions about clothes, parties, money, and even boys? Why do you think she is such close friends with Mimi and Divine, despite their differences?

8. It's important to Rhyann to wait until marriage before having sex. Do you think her aunt is right in worrying that Rhyann will slip up? Rhyann worries that Mimi is being manipulated by Kyle. Do you foresee trouble for her?

9. Mimi accuses Rhyann of being negative, to which Rhyann replies that she's only being realistic. In what respect do you think Rhyann is down-to-earth, and in what areas is she just closed off and scared? How do you think Mrs. Goldberg's final wishes and letter will affect Rhyann's outlook in the future?

10. From the beginning of *It's a Curl Thing*, Rhyann has experienced many difficulties and sorrows. What tragedies and struggles has she had to live through? What is her

tone in discussing her mother's death and the neighborhood in which she lives? Why do you think Mrs. Goldberg's death affects her so deeply? How does it help her to face her grief over losing her mother and aunt?

ACTIVITIES TO ENHANCE YOUR BOOK CLUB

1. Rhyann, Divine, and Mimi are all able to learn more about the experiences of victims of the Holocaust by reaching out via the internet and going to museums, such as the Museum of Tolerance in Los Angeles. You can also research to learn more. Read some of the books dealing with the Holocaust mentioned in *It's a Curl Thing*, such as *Valaida*, by Candace Allen, or *If You Save One Life*, by Eva Brown.

2. Plan a trip to the hair salon with your book club. While you're there, share your own hair disaster stories.

3. For more about the author, check out her websites at www.jacquelinthomas.com and www.simplydivine books.com.

Pocket Books
Proudly Presents

Split Ends

Coming Fall 2009

$\mathcal{I}$ swallow my pride and hold my breath as I rummage through the crumpled, grease-stained fast-food wrappers, coffee cups, and unrecognizable stuff in the trash area across the street from the Crowning Glory Hair Salon. I promised Miss Lucy I would bring some cans back with me when we meet back at the mission.

I back away from the trash, gasping for a whiff of fresh air. I honestly don't know how she does it, going through stinky trash cans daily. I can't wait to find the nearest public bathroom to wash my hands.

I glance over my shoulder in time to see a girl around my age walk out of the Crowning Glory Salon. I have seen her going in and out a few times so I'm guessing that she works there.

She stops just outside the shop and looks in my direction.

I am so embarrassed right now that I wish the ground would open up and swallow me. She has already seen me picking through the trash so there is no point in running off. Instead, I pretend that I'm not aware she's staring me down, hoping she'll have the good sense to just move on, but she doesn't. Instead she walks to the end of the sidewalk and heads in my direction.

I look down at my stained T-shirt and torn blue jeans, then up at her starched and pressed denim, her eye-popping pink shirt and matching bangles. She has her chin-length hair neatly pulled back in a ponytail.

As she comes closer, a wave of apprehension washes over me and for an instant, I consider taking off running, but for some reason I can't make my feet move.

I sure hope that she is not a whack job or anything. I don't know her and she might be the type who can't stand homeless people. The last thing I need is a beat-down from a complete stranger. She might think I've been trying to case the shop or something.

I look up, meeting her gaze without a flinch. If she's comes here trying to get in my face—I'll get with her, no problem.

She looks a little uncomfortable so I speak first. "Hey."

"Hey," she responds back, eyeing me from head to toe. "I'm Rhyann. I've seen you around here a few times and I want to give you this," she states, holding out five or six dollar bills and a five.

She probably thinks I need the money more than she does, which I do, but I hate the look of pity I see in her eyes. I survey her nice jeans and silk shirt. Her sandals are fierce. I only own a pair of four-dollar flip-flops. When I left home, I only took what I could fit in my backpack. Right now, she is eyeing my raggedy Converse sneakers.

"It's not much, but it'll get you something to eat," she tells me. "I wish it was more." She steals a peek over my shoulder before adding, "Some of the clients today were a little on the cheap side when it came to tipping."

I smile and she smiles back.

I don't want to take her money, but I'm pure tired after

looking for cans all up and down the street. Miss Lucy and I do have to eat when we're not at the Safe Harbor Mission.

"Thank you," I say after a moment, taking the money out of her hand. "I appreciate it. Oh, my name is Kylie." I really am grateful because I was struggling with going through those nasty trash cans. I'm sure Miss Lucy won't hold it against me if I bring home money instead.

"Do you have somewhere to stay?" she asks me.

I nod. "If I leave now, I can get a bed at the mission."

"Stay safe," she replies. "I hear it can get pretty bad out there."

"Thank you, Rhyann."

I turn and break into a sprint down the sidewalk. I am supposed to meet Miss Lucy in about an hour and I need to get to the bus stop.

The bus arrives fifteen minutes after I get there. It's hotter than a two-dollar pistol, as Grandma Ellen used to say. And I'm sweating bullets.

I get on and find a seat near the back, humming softly and relieved that I didn't have to rummage further through those foul-smelling trash cans. The stench from the trash mingled with my perspiration is a stinky combination.

Miss Lucy is waiting for me when I step off the bus thirty minutes later. "Did you talk to that lady about your hair?" she asks me.

"No, ma'am. She's been having a lot of customers in the morning. I think I need to go down there before eight."

"Maybe you should try later on in the day," Miss Lucy suggests. "After dinner, we need to take those things out of your head."

"I met this girl that works there and she gave me some

money," I say. "I felt funny taking it, but I knew that we could use a few dollars."

"That was real nice of her."

"She's my age, I think, and seems very nice."

"Sounds like it if she gave you her tips," Miss Lucy states. "You should've asked her about getting your hair washed."

"I didn't think about it at the time. I was shocked that she even approached me like that."

Miss Lucy wipes her face with a sweat-stained rag she keeps in her cart. "I have a feeling that it's going to be a real hot summer."

"I'ma go see if I can take a shower, Miss Lucy." Screwing up my face, I add, "I stink."

"I'll be in the TV room," she tells me.

When I come out, Miss Lucy unzips her backpack and takes out a sock, handing it to me along with a safety pin.

"What is this for?" I ask.

"Put your money in there," Miss Lucy advises in a loud whisper. "Try not to keep change. Convert it to dollar bills as soon as you can. Never keep more than a dollar or two out. Keep the rest of it in the sock and pin it to your bra or your underwear. Don't ever let anyone see that you have money or where you keep it. When people lose hope and are desperate, they're liable to do anything."

"Yes, ma'am."

"Go on to the bathroom and hide your money," she whispers. Miss Lucy glances around the room before adding, "Make sure when we're talking that nobody else is around."

"Yes, ma'am," I say a second time before excusing myself.

I walk inside the bathroom and stash the money inside the sock as Miss Lucy instructed and then pin it to the waist of my underwear. It feels weird, but it beats hiding money in the socks I wear. The weather is really warm and I'd rather be walking around in my flip-flops.

"You got it straight?"

I smile at Miss Lucy and respond, "Yes, ma'am."

"Good."

We notice that people are starting to gather around the building.

"Must be time for dinner," Miss Lucy says. "We better get in line, too. I already got our vouchers."

Inside and outside of the mission is a long line of people standing around. Some talk loudly, often using R-rated language, complaining about life or the quality of the food we are served or some rule or two that they don't agree with.

Others line up at the window to receive their meal ticket and some smoke on the steps right outside the entrance. They are the disabled, mentally ill, drug addicted, or working poor who cannot afford an apartment in a city with few housing options for low-income people.

Mostly, we just wait.

The faint odor of sweat and grime, a by-product of living on the streets, neutralizes the aromas floating from the kitchen.

"The showers are free," Miss Lucy states. "I don't know why they won't use them." Families with children are placed in separate dormitories—I guess this is where my mama and me will eventually end up. I met a girl whose parents both have jobs, but are living in a shelter until they can afford housing.

"There are two types of people here in this place," Miss Lucy tells me when I mention that to her. "There are those who are here just for three hots and a cot. The others are here for soup, soap, and hope. It's up to you to decide which group you belong to."

"I want the soup, soap, and hope," I say as we enter the

dining hall. "I hope for a normal life and for my mama to finally grow up. That's all I really want." I pause a moment before adding, "Oh, and I want to go back to school. I don't want to be a high school dropout. It's a tough row to hoe if you don't graduate from high school."

I drop my backpack on an empty chair. "I'ma leave this here."

"Kylie, you have to be careful with your stuff," Miss Lucy says, picking up the backpack. "You put your teeth down and they'll steal them. And just so you know . . . there are some people here with psychiatric problems which can negatively affect others, so fights often break out."

"I'll be careful," I say.

We get our dinner and search for empty spaces at one of the tables. A lady waves to get our attention. Miss Lucy and I join her at a table. Tonight we have fried chicken, coleslaw, baked beans, and a roll. I passed on some of the other selections while Miss Lucy says that she doesn't turn down anything.

After dinner, and after claiming our beds, we venture to the TV room, where a rerun of *The Cosby Show* is on. I sit down on the floor in front of Miss Lucy.

I feel a touch of sadness, as my grandma would say, while watching the happy, loving family life displayed onscreen. I've never met my father. My mama told me that his family moved away after they found out she was pregnant.

There have been times that I've been tempted to try and find him, but then I change my mind because I can't handle more rejection. Although there are times I dream of my father coming to find me. I dream that he has been searching for me all these years and when we finally meet, he can't say much because he's crying.

"What are you thinking about?" Miss Lucy whispers in my ear.

"I was thinking about my father. I've never met him."

"That's a shame," she murmurs. "I didn't know my daddy, either. He took off shortly after I was born. I was told by his family that he died a year later, but to be honest, we never knew if that was true or not. My mother told us when we were older that he ran off with another man's wife. She believed that he faked his death so no one would come looking for him."

"Sometimes I think I want to get married and have my own family, but when I hear stuff like that—I really don't know," I tell her. "Maybe it's best to just be alone."

Miss Lucy shakes her head no. "No, baby. I don't think we were born to be alone in this world. We just have to trust God to guide us to the right people in our lives."

"That's what Grandma Ellen used to say. It's not that I want to be alone, really. I just don't want to marry some man, and after I have his children, he ups and decides he doesn't love me. I don't want to be a single parent. It's too hard."

"You just keep that in mind every time you meet a young man. Boys today are ready to get in your panties before they even know your name. They will tell you whatever you want to hear to get what they want."

I agree. "They can't get nothing from me. I'm not falling for all that fast talk. I know better because I see what it does to my mama."

"It's easy to coach from the sidelines," Miss Lucy says to me.

I frown. "What do you mean by that?"

"That it's easier to say what you won't do when you're not directly involved. When some young man catches your eye, you don't know how you will respond."

"I'm not gonna go monkeying around with nobody. I don't care what he tells me. It ain't that kind of party."

Miss Lucy gives me a big grin. "One day I just might remind you of those words."

I notice a couple of girls around my age in the TV room. One looks like she really doesn't want to be bothered, so I get up and approach the other girl. She's a runaway who left Texas to be an actress.

"I have been taking acting lessons since I was six years old," she tells me. "But then my mother remarries and decides that I should focus on getting a college education. Her new husband is a college professor."

"So you don't have any family here?" I inquire.

"Naw," she responds, trying to act all highfalutin. Somebody needs to tell this chick that she is in a homeless shelter. "Hollywood is where I need to be if I'm gonna be an actress, Kylie. I just didn't think it would be so hard."

"What about school?"

"I just graduated. I'm gonna get me a job waitressing in a club or a bar so that my days are free for auditions." She tosses her dirty-blond hair across her shoulder. "My father is sending me some money on Friday. He has to sell off some stock. I'm using that to get an apartment."

"That's good. I'm happy for you, Laura," I say. Deep down, I hope that she is telling the truth and isn't living in a fantasy world in her head. "I hope to see you on the big screen one day."

She breaks into a smile. "I hope so, too. If I don't make it as an actress, then I'm gonna try film school."

"It sounds like you have a plan."

Laura nods. "But I really want to be an actress. That's my dream."

"My grandma used to tell me to never give up on my dreams, so don't give up on your dream, Laura."

"Hey, you wanna get an apartment together?"

"I don't have any money," I tell her. "I have to find a job, too. Besides, I can't just up and leave Miss Lucy. She's my guardian."

She looks disappointed. "Oh . . . okay."

Miss Lucy rises to her feet and waves to let me know that she is going off to bed.

"Is that her? Your guardian?" Laura asks me.

"Yeah, that's her."

"How did you two end up here?"

"We fell on hard times," I state. "That's about it—our story is no different from anybody else's story."

"Have you met Jasmina?"

I shake my head no. "Who is that?"

"That girl sitting over there. She's a runaway," Laura tells me. "She came from northern California. She's pregnant and her boyfriend dumped her when he found out. She was afraid to tell her parents, so she left home."

Laura gestures for Jasmina to join us.

When she comes over, Laura introduces us. "Hey, Jasmina," I say. "Nice to meet you."

"Nice to meet you, too," she responds.

We sit in the TV room for the next two hours talking about everything from Hollywood celebrities we would like to meet to favorite movies to boys.

I stifle my yawn. "I don't know about y'all, but I'm getting sleepy. I'll see you in the morning."

I overhear Jasmina and Laura make plans to have breakfast together. They seem to be building a friendship. Maybe they should consider becoming roommates.

Miss Lucy is asleep and snoring softly when I tiptoe over to my bed. I climb in and pull the covers up to my chin, my backpack in my arms.

My eyelids feel heavier than a pig in a knapsack. The clock on the wall reads 11:10. It's the last thing I remember before waking up shortly after 7:00 a.m.

I sit up, giving my eyes time to adjust to the morning light. I take my backpack and head to the bathrooms to wash up.

When I come out a few minutes later, a line of women is beginning to form, all wanting to wash away as much of the grime and stench of homelessness off their bodies as they can. They long to feel human again.

A person of worth.

Even at my age, I can totally understand what that feels like.

I wake Miss Lucy up.

She groans.

"Wake up, Miss Lucy," I say in a low voice. "You need to get up now."

She opens her eyes. "My body hurts something fierce."

"Do you want me to see if they have any Tylenol or something?"

She nods.

Miss Lucy normally has her aches and pains throughout the day, but this time she really looks like she is in agony.

Worried, I run off to speak to one of the workers.

"Do you have any Tylenol? My guardian needs some kind of pain medication really bad. It's Miss Lucy and she's in a lot of pain."

The woman named Carol responds, "I have some. I will go and check on Lucy. Why don't you get in line to get breakfast and have them fix Lucy's plate, too?"

"Thanks."

I get in line behind Jasmina and Laura.

"Good morning," I say.

"Morning," they respond in unison.

"How long did y'all stay up?" I inquire.

"For about an hour," Jasmina replies with a yawn. "What are you doing today?"

"I'm gonna take the bus over to Sunset Boulevard. I want to check out some stuff and hopefully find a job."

"I was thinking about trying to find something close by so that I can walk to work." Jasmina picked up a tray and handed it to me, then picked up another for her. "I need to have a place by the time my baby is born."

"Have you considered telling your parents?" I ask. "You need medical care."

"Kylie, if I thought they could handle it, I'd still be home with them. They are going to be so upset."

"I bet they're upset now because they don't know where you are." I pick up two bowls of fruit.

Miss Lucy walks up to me and I get her a tray. "Here's your fruit."

Jasmina grabs a bagel. "I miss my parents, Kylie."

"They love you so I think they'll understand and support you," I respond. "Just call them and give them a chance."

"Why did you run away?" she asks me.

"My mama didn't want to be a mom. If she did, I'd be home. You have two parents who truly love you. Give them a chance. Just think about what I've said."

I take my food over to a nearby table and sit down.

Miss Lucy takes a seat across from me. "That was some good advice you gave that young lady."

I glance up, meeting Miss Lucy's gaze. "Only you think that I should take it myself, don't you?"

She gave a slight shrug. "I didn't say that."

"But it's what you think I should do."

Miss Lucy finishes off her fruit. "All I can tell you is to let the Lord lead you, Kylie."

I take a sip of my apple juice. "Miss Lucy, I'm gonna go back over to Sunset around eleven. I'll help you look for cans before I go."

"Why are you going so late?"

I shrug. "I don't know. I guess it's because I haven't had any luck going there in the mornings, so I figure I'll try your suggestion. If this doesn't work, then I'm not going back. It's a waste of money."

"Well, I guess it can't hurt," Miss Lucy says to me.

"If I can't speak with her today, then I'm gonna give up and just try and take the braids out myself."

"I told you that I'd help you as much as I can get these fingers to work."

"I have to do something or go bald this year."

Miss Lucy chuckles. "You would be a pretty little bald-headed girl."

"Naaw," I utter. "I don't think so. I may not be much of a fashionista, but I do believe hair is a wonderful accessory and one I don't want to be without. I would rather get stuck with needles all day long than go without a strand of hair on my head. I already know that I am probably going to have to get it cut—I'm okay with that—but I don't want my hair so short that I look like a boy."

I stare at this one dress in the boutique window every time I come over here to Sunset Boulevard. It is a beautiful purple color and I love it, but it's not something I would ever really buy unless it went on sale for like ninety percent off. I know that my mama would love this store. She likes anything with a designer label attached to it.

I spot Rhyann, the girl who gave me her tips, a few yards ahead of me. Almost as if she senses my presence, she turns around and our eyes meet.

She waves and I wave back.

Rhyann stops in her tracks and looks as if she is waiting on me, so I walk quickly to catch up to her.

"Hey, how are you?" she asks.

"I'm okay," I respond, biting my bottom lip.

People passing by begin staring at us. I'm sure we probably look strange standing here talking like this, but Rhyann doesn't seem to care.

"Have you eaten?" she asks.

"I had breakfast at the mission."

Rhyann holds up a sandwich from Subway. "I just ate half of this sandwich and I'm full. I don't know why I bought a 12-inch in the first place. You can have it if you want."

I don't respond.

"Look, I'm not offering this to you out of pity or anything like that, if that's what you're thinking."

"Then why are you doing it?" I ask out of curiosity. "You don't know me."

"You're right, I don't, but that doesn't stop me from caring what happens to you."

"Do you help all homeless people you see?" I ask.

"No, but it's not because I don't want to," she answers. "I don't have a lot of money myself. Still, it just bothers me when I see someone my age out here on the streets. I live over near the Jungle—it's crazy over there and I'm in a house. I can't imagine being on the streets."

I give her a tiny smile. My mama and I didn't live far from the Jungle, either. We were always hearing gunshots or police sirens and helicopters in that area.

She's still holding her sandwich out to me.

"Are you sure you don't want it?" I inquire. "You might get hungry later."

"I'm not big on leftovers," Rhyann confesses. "Most likely it will get thrown away."

"Thank you," I say as I take the sub from her. "I appreciate it."

"You're welcome," she responds, then says, "You should come into the salon and let Miss Marilee or China wash your hair. They can do it early in the morning or after we close."

"That's why I've been hanging around here," I confess. "I'm usually here around nine or so, but she's been getting a lot of customers coming in at that time."

"Would you like to come with me now?"

I shake my head no and say, "Rhyann, I can't go in that place looking like this."

"Is it okay if I tell her to expect you tomorrow morning?" she asks me. "That way she won't make an early appointment. I know that she doesn't have one until ten."

"You would do that for me?"

She nods. "I'm sure you want to get your hair done over or at least get the rest of those braids out."

"I've been trying to take them out by myself."

"Come tomorrow morning," Rhyann tells me. "Try to be here right at eight."

"Are you sure it'll be okay with her?"

Rhyann nodded. "Miss Marilee will do it. Girl, she's nice like that. Just take out as many of the braids as you can. I won't be there in the morning, but I will let her know that you'll be coming by."

"You like working there?" I want to know.

Rhyann nods. "Yeah. It's a cool place to work. Everybody is nice. I only work part-time. I could probably do full-time, but I like going to the beach during the summer with my friends."

"That sounds nice," I say, wishing I had a group of friends to hang out with, period.

Rhyann checks her watch. "I need to get back to work, but make sure you come tomorrow."

"I'll be here," I vow. "Rhyann, thanks for everything."

"I won't be here in the morning, but I hope I'll see you again. Real soon."

I smile. "Me too."

I watch her until she disappears in the crowd and then make my way to the bus stop, humming softly.

"You might as well stop spending money to go over to Sunset if you're not gonna get something done to that head of yours," Miss Lucy tells me when I meet up with her forty-five minutes later.

"I'm gonna get it done tomorrow morning. I have an appointment."

Her eyes grow wide in her surprise. "You talked to the owner?"

I shake my head no. "I didn't talk to her, but I did see Rhyann. She is the girl I told you about. She told me that Miss Marilee didn't have any appointments until ten and that she would tell her to expect me around eight o'clock."

"Good for you," Miss Lucy replies. "I know how much you want to get those braids out."

"I'm gonna try to take more out tonight."

We walk over to the dormitory where the families are housed until they can find a more permanent place to live. Miss Lucy wants to read to the children. I go with her because it's not like I have anything else to do.

While she reads, I help in the nursery with the babies. I didn't know that I could volunteer. For me, this is a way to pay them back for what they are doing for me. A few of the volunteers know my name and always stop to see how I'm doing.

My mama crosses my mind because she was supposed to go to court. She probably didn't bother showing up, like she always do. If she is evicted, I won't know where she is or if she leaves town. I may never see my mama again.

I'm not so sure how I feel about that.

She works my last nerve and all, but I don't want her to totally disappear from my life.

"Miss Lucy, I'll be right back," I say when I spot a public phone. "I need to make a phone call."

"Okay. I'll be over there," she says, pointing across the street. "I see some cans."

Biting my bottom lip, I navigate to the phone.

What if the number has been disconnected? How do I find my mama?

I breathe a sigh of relief when I hear the ringing on the other end instead of a recording.

"Hello."

I'm shocked when my mama answers.

"Hello, who is this?" she asks. "Kylie, is this you?"

I don't say anything.

"Kylie honey, just say something please," she begs. "I know it's you. Look, everything is fine. Clyde paid the rent for us so that we can stay in the apartment. Of course, he's moving in, but it's only to help us out. You can come on back home. We don't have to move."

I sigh in frustration. Why would I want to go back there with some thug living in the apartment?

"It's just temporary," Mama quickly interjects. "Kylie, why won't you talk to me? Tell me where you are? Honey, say something . . ."

"I just called to see if you were okay," I state. "And to let you know that I'm okay. I don't want you to worry about me."

Not that you were.

"You need to come home, Kylie."

"Mama, who is Clyde?" I ask her.

"He's my man."

"What happened to Jake?" I question. "I haven't been gone that long. When did you meet Clyde?"

"Kylie, I really like this guy. Come home so that you can meet him. I just know we're gonna be one big happy family."

"I don't think so," I say. "But I'm glad you weren't evicted. Mama, I need to get off this phone."

"Kylie . . ."

"'Bye, Mama."

"Tell me where you've been living. I want to know how to reach you." I hang up the phone, fighting back tears.

Want more teen fiction fun?
Check out these titles:

LaVergne, TN USA
26 September 2010
198541LV00004B/8/P